I0750510

THE SANCTUARY

THE CAPTIVE SERIES

DANIELLE BANNISTER

THE SANCTUARY

DANIELLE
BANNISTER

CITY OWL
PRESS

This book is a work of fiction. Names, characters, places, and incidents either are products of the author's imagination or are used fictitiously. Any resemblance to actual events or locales or persons, living or dead, is entirely coincidental and not intended by the author.

THE SANCTUARY
The Captive, Book 3
By: Danielle Bannister

CITY OWL PRESS
www.cityowlpress.com

Cover Design by MiblArt. All stock photos licensed appropriately.

Edited by Tina Moss.

For information on subsidiary rights, please contact the publisher at info@cityowlpress.com.

Print Edition ISBN: 978-1-64898-544-7

Digital Edition ISBN: 978-1-64898-543-0

Printed in the United States of America

ALSO BY DANIELLE BANNISTER

THE ROMANCES

The Sweeter Side

The ABCs of Dee

Doppelganger

Must Love Coffee

Taking Stock

What Moons Do (YA)

Waiting in the Wings

Waiting on the Words

The Sexier Side

The First 100 Kisses

The Second 100 Kisses

Where You Left Me-Vol. 1-5

FANTASY AND PARANORMAL

The Hallowed Realms Trilogy with Amy Miles

The Lurkers Within: A Havenwood Falls Novella

The Twin Flames Trilogy

DARK ROMANCE AND THRILLER

Girl On Fire

The Cage

The Safehouse

The Sanctuary

PRAISE FOR DANIELLE BANNISTER

"Bannister weaved a gripping tale with an original concept making *Pulled* a very enjoyable read. I was never quite sure where the author would direct her characters, what the outcome would be which I really liked. And the final outcome was certainly not what I expected, so bravo!"

— *Two Nerds with Words*

"Reading books from authors that you have read before and you think you know their style of writing, and then BAM!!! They go and write something that is completely off the wall for them, you end up loving that author just a little bit more."

— *Kelly's Nerdy Obsession*

"*The ABC's of Dee* was funny and engaging from the first page. I loved being inside Dee's head as she navigated her hilarious dating adventures. She was honest with herself almost to a fault, but her ongoing inner commentary was refreshing and relatable."

— *Avid Reader*

"*The First 100 Kisses* is Bannister's next standalone. I loved every minute of it! The characters are a great match. Complete opposites. The lessons went from sweet to sinful. It was perfect."

— *Two Book Pushers*

"Holy mac and cheese, or should I say burgers and fries *wink* , *The Second 100 Kisses* is just everything to me right now!! A perfect balance of swoon, smexy, comedy, drama, angst, and character building...all while keeping it real. I devoured these books in one sitting and both left me with all the feels."

— *Book Flirts*

This book is dedicated to one of my very best friends, Kelly Hewins. Fuck cancer.

AUTHOR'S NOTE

This book is the third in a series. Before you read *The Sanctuary*, you need to read *The Cage* and *The Safehouse* or you will be very confused.

RECAP OF THE CAGE AND THE SAFEHOUSE

The Sanctuary is book three in The Captive Series. If it has been a minute since you read *The Cage* and *The Safehouse* and can't quite remember what it's about, here are the rough points to remember. You are welcome to skip the recap.

RECAP of *The Cage*

- Connor runs an illegal "pet" adoption agency, aka a human trafficking ring.
- Amanda was tricked into his ring under the promise of a rental unit. A unit she was then locked inside of while Connor prepped her for sale.
- Amanda, using her only weapon against Connor—her feminine prowess—must convince him that he loves her so that he won't sell her off.
- In her bid for survival, the line between who Connor is and who he could be is blurred. Her emotions get jumbled. Does she like Connor or is it just survival instincts?
- Connor, afraid of his own feelings for one of his "pets" tries to sell her off to a guy named Malcolm. A guy,

ironically, Amanda knew from her childhood, under a different name.

- Malcolm quickly realizes Amanda is not with Connor of her own free will and takes it upon himself to free Amanda by stealing her away.
- Connor finds out that Malcolm has taken his property and goes after him.
- *The Cage* ends with Malcolm and Amanda fleeing with Connor close on their heels.

RECAP of *The Safehouse*

- Malcolm drives Amanda across the country, trying to hide their identities from cameras and Connor's goons who might be on the lookout for them. They both cut their hair. Amanda dyes her hair black and Malcolm shaves his beard.
- During their escape to a safehouse across the country, Amanda and Malcolm grow close.
- Connor discovers their plan to escape and has his men on the hunt for them. His underground network helps him find out their final destination in New Hampshire.
- Sexual tension mounts between Amanda and Malcolm as the forced proximity messes with both of their libidos, but Malcolm won't have sex with her because he knows she's been through too much trauma. That doesn't mean they don't mess around quite a bit.
- Connor catches up with the unknowing duo. Amanda quickly pulls a fast one on Malcolm to keep him safe. She roofies him, hides Malcolm in the panic room, and gives herself over to Connor, coming up with a back story that she hopes he will believe.
- Connor takes Amanda back to her original cage, and Malcolm flees.

- Back at Connor's encampment, Amanda learns that Kelli and the other girls are still trapped. She's done nothing to help anyone. Her only saving grace is that she protected Malcolm from Connor's wrath.
- Malcolm makes his way back and breaks into Connor's building. While hiding in the basement, he trips the alarms so the fire department will come and investigate. Connor doubles down on Malcolm's play by setting the place on fire. Connor leaves Amanda in her cage to die in the flames, opting to save himself.
- When Malcolm discovers Connor in the parking garage, he has a choice: take Connor down or save Amanda. He chooses the latter.
- Together, Malcolm and Amanda run again to a new safehouse, but Amanda feels awful knowing the other girls didn't make it out alive.
- *The Safehouse* ends from Kelli's point of view and her savior, Holden, an undercover cop who was working to take down the sex ring.

CHAPTER ONE

AMANDA

It had been weeks of traveling to get as far away from Connor as possible, and I still couldn't get the smell of smoke out of my nose. It lingered everywhere, as though it were embedded in my skin, tattooed on my fingertips, and coated in my hair, despite countless showers. I could never seem to shake the scent.

My bones were weary. Malcolm said it was no wonder with all the travel we'd done, constantly shifting in planes, cars, and taxis. It had been nothing but non-stop movement to avoid detection. Neither one of us had gotten much rest. Yet, what I felt... was restless. Even when we stopped moving, I wouldn't be at peace. I'd forever be looking over my shoulder. I hated that I'd damned Malcolm to that same burden. It wouldn't matter where we went. We'd never be safe.

Not while Connor was alive.

Despite that knowledge, I knew I should be grateful. I was alive. I was out of Connor's cage. And I was with someone who would try his best to keep me safe. I wasn't burned alive like the woman who had been left caged in the fire. Nor was I damned like Kelli, who was likely being used for sick and twisted mutilation fetishes. I got out... but I was still trapped.

Was this how I was going to have to live out my days? Always on the move, forever in disguise, never lingering for long in the outside world?

That wasn't a life. It was a prison sentence.

"We should be landing in twenty minutes," Malcolm said from his seat beside me. He wore a dark baseball hat and glasses with no prescription. His beard was still gone as was the light that used to live in his eyes.

I didn't respond to him. He didn't expect me to. I'd barely spoken since the fire. With so much to process, I was working overtime trying to dodge feeling any of it.

"This is our last flight," Malcolm continued. "Just a short drive, and we'll be at our final destination."

It wouldn't be, though. We'd have to run again, once Connor's thugs caught wind of us. We might have a respite, but there would be no peace. Not while Connor breathed.

"Amanda..." Malcolm tried. He looked as drained as I felt. The dark circles under his eyes rivaled my own. The blond wig I wore for this trip made my scalp itch. I wanted nothing more than to rip it off and chuck it at the teenager popping his gum incessantly in the seat in front of us. But I wasn't stupid. We were flying coach. Private planes would have been too easy to spot. We needed to blend into the scenery. We'd managed to slip under the radar so far. How long could we keep it up?

Malcolm figured Connor would go underground, especially with the authorities investigating what had been happening inside his apartment building. That might have been well and good, but Connor had hired hands. And they would have orders to take down their target, no matter where Connor was.

"I know this has been hard on you." Malcolm ran a hand through his hair. "Once we get you settled, I'll arrange to have a therapist come and—"

At that, I snorted. "A therapist? You think a shrink is going to fix all the twisted shit I've been through?"

"I think it's a start. Therapy is a good tool to use when dealing with huge life events. The woman I spoke to after my mother's passing was—"

I clicked my teeth. "No thanks. I don't want to regurgitate anything from the last few weeks. Okay? I want to forget it all happened."

He shook his head. "Suppressing your trauma isn't healthy."

"Yeah, well reliving it certainly isn't going to be a walk in the park. Drop it. No therapy. If you don't want to deal with this shit, I totally understand. Just leave me at the airport. I'll find a way. I always do." I sighed and pinched my eyes together to hold back the tears threatening to fall.

"I'm not abandoning you, Amanda."

I turned and stared him dead in the eyes. "You should. You should have let me go the first time I tried to run. Now, we're both fucked."

"I would hardly call my situation 'fucked.' I quite enjoy spending time with you, in case you didn't notice." He shot me a tired grin. "Besides, I'm a recluse. I hate most people. I can happily live out my days outside of the real world, if I get to share that time with you. And it won't be forever. Just until the police catch Connor. And they will. They'll find all the evidence of his crimes. They will find him, prosecute him, put him in jail, and throw away the key."

"You think a judicial system Connor has bought and paid for is going to lock him up?" I leaned back against the plane's unforgiving headrest. "You're delusional."

He crossed his arms over his chest. "He hasn't bought everyone out. Having a few local cops wherever he sets up shop is one thing, but to assume he has every jurisdiction in his pocket is highly unlikely."

"Unlikely, but not impossible." I shifted in my seat, giving him my back and signaling the conversation was over. He was trying to dish out hope, claiming a light at the end of the tunnel. But I knew better. At the end of the tunnel, there was just another tunnel. Darker than the one before it.

"Wake up, Amanda. We're here."

I opened my eyes to discover yet another cab interior. I'd lost track of how many we'd been in and out of the last several days. It was dark outside. I couldn't see much of anything. Even so, it felt oddly familiar.

"Where is here?" I asked as I unbuckled my seatbelt. Malcolm didn't answer until the cab had left us on the curb with the two suitcases we'd been living out of.

"My house. Where Connor first tried to sell you to me."

My blood ran cold. "We have been traveling for *days* only to return to the same place we left. Are you insane?"

"The travel was to get him off our scent. Think about it, Amanda. It's the perfect spot. It's the last place he'd think we'd go. No one in their right mind would return to where it began."

"You're not in your right mind, that's for sure," I huffed, searching over my shoulder. This was not a good idea.

Malcolm, sensing my stress, put his hands on my shoulders to steady me. "We'll live on the lower level. No windows there. We'll leave the upper levels as abandoned as they have been. From the outside, it'll look like the property is vacant." He picked up the suitcases. "No one will know we're here. Trust me. Let's get inside before the sun comes up."

I stood my ground. "Malcolm, this is madness. He will be monitoring your place... There could be someone in the bushes right now!"

"There isn't. I have security cameras. There has been no trace of anyone. Besides, Connor's goons will have scattered now that the authorities are sniffing around. Connor is not in a position to be giving orders right now. He will have to go dark. This is the best time to take shelter. And this is my strongest safehouse, Amanda. It's the perfect spot to lay low until he's caught."

"*If* he gets caught," I corrected.

Malcolm frowned. "I know you think this is crazy, but I do know a thing or two about hiding from people you don't want to find you." He dropped one of the suitcases and raised a hand to his chest. "Fellow black-market criminal here, don't forget. I've hidden out in this house dozens of times in my career. It's well stocked for our needs. Now, let's go." He took my hand, and I let him lead me into another cage.

MALCOLM

Coming back to the Seattle house was a huge gamble. The largest gamble of my life. It wasn't the first time Connor had tried to reach me at this address. He'd done it with the video of Kelli's finger and for the picture of Amanda giving Connor head. So, to risk coming back to the place Connor or his thugs had been to multiple times wasn't wise. What I'd told Amanda, however, was true. This was my safest lockdown location. We could live here for months undetected.

But there was another reason I wanted to come back.

In the time we'd been traveling, Darcy informed me of another message arriving on my doorstep. This new message, however, seemed to be from someone named H. Darcy had told me about a cryptic message that was couriered to my house.

It read: *Gwen is safe. Need to talk. Bring A.* It had a street address I didn't know. Of course, I didn't trust a word of it. The message had to be from Connor or one of his men. But to sniff out anything, I needed access to my network. And my best setup was in the Seattle house. Once I discovered more about the message's origin, I'd fill Amanda in. Until then, there was no need to get her upset.

Once Amanda was inside the house, I locked the doors, re-engaged the security system, and directed her straight to the basement. Access to the lower level was via a hidden door on the floor. The couch slid out and the narrow stairway, wide enough for one person, appeared.

"You have stairs under your couch?" she asked.

I grinned. "You don't?"

She rolled her eyes at my bad attempt to lighten the mood, but she made her way down the stairs. I rolled the couch into place over my head, hiding our descent from view. The darkness overtook the small stairwell once the floor was locked into place.

I grabbed my burner cell and flicked on the flashlight. I held it up to a locked door at the bottom of the stairs. To the right of the door was the keypad. I typed in my code as Amanda watched me.

"ALuxx 1005?" She raised a quizzical eyebrow. "What does the 'A' stand for? Let me guess? Middle initial?"

The door unlocked.

I shrugged. "It's no secret I've had a crush on you for decades. You know what they say, manifest what you want. Well, teenage me wanted you. Your name, combined with mine, is part of just about every password I have." I realized how much that said about me.

She looked at me, seemingly unfazed by my ridiculousness. "And the one thousand and five? What's that mean?"

"It's a date. October fifth."

"A date marking what?"

I closed my eyes. "Our wedding day. It's the perfect temperature for an outdoor fall wedding."

"You've been manifesting our wedding day in your passwords?"

"Everyone needs a hobby."

Amanda blinked at me. "I don't know if I should feel flattered or freaked out."

"Probably both is advisable, considering I'm about to lock you in a basement." I regretted the joke as soon as I said it. "Sorry, that was in poor taste."

"But nonetheless true." Amanda walked inside, and the motion sensor lights came on. She glanced around the space. From her expression, I could tell she was picturing a typical American basement: musty scents, surrounded by cement walls and fluorescent lighting. My hideout was anything but a stereotype.

"Are these... hardwood floors? In a basement?" She bent to touch it. "Oh, my God, it's real wood. I thought it must be laminate." Her eyes caught something across the room. "There's a bar? You have a bar? And a fireplace?" She went over to the large black fireplace, which ran the entire width of the living room. Touching the space above the fireplace, she gasped. "That's water. You have a waterfall fireplace?"

"I do. And there is a projection screen that drops from the ceiling for movies." I pointed to the slot just above the fireplace.

"Of course you do." She peered at the large seating area. "Leather couches? Jesus, Malcolm, this ottoman could double as a bed. It's massive."

"That's what she said."

That earned me a throw-pillow to the chest. Worth it.

"How many bedrooms?" she asked, looking around to spot them.

"Just the one, I'm afraid. But if you'd prefer, I could sleep on the ottoman."

"Wise ass." She searched the place a bit more, lifting items and marveling at the opulence.

I'd spent quite a fortune designing it, but if you had to lock yourself away from society for any amount of time, you didn't want to feel like you were in a prison.

When she disappeared into the master bedroom, she shrieked. I ran instantly to her side, fists at the ready, only to see that she'd climbed inside the tub. A huge smile graced her lips.

"You have a claw foot tub!" she squealed. "I have *always* wanted a claw foot tub."

"I know."

She cocked her head. "You know?"

"You told me about your dream house over lunch at school one day. Don't you remember?"

"I did?"

I nodded. "Yes. You said you loved real hardwood flooring and drooled over your neighbor's leather sofas—"

"And that people who owned fireplaces were 'the shit,'" Amanda whispered. "Malcolm, did you design *my* dream house?"

I kicked at the floor sheepishly. "How'd I do?"

The shock of my borderline-obsessive behavior spread across her face. She shifted in the tub so she was kneeling in front of me. "Take your pants off."

"I'm sorry?" I asked, not sure I'd heard her right.

"I'm going to suck you off." She grabbed at my pants.

"Amanda, that's not necessary. I've told you. I'm not going to use you like that."

"No, I'm using you. Malcolm, no man has *ever* listened to what I have wanted. Ever." Her hands slid down my thighs. "You? You built me a fucking living space based on some random conversation we had when we were seventeen. That means something to me. And I want to show you my appreciation."

I put my hands over hers. "Just your being here with me shows me that, Amanda."

"Pants. Off. Now."

As much as I wanted to object to her demand, my cock had heard her order the first time and was already rising to the occasion. We'd have to have another discussion about her feeling the need to repay my help with sexual favors, but that conversation would need to happen later... when my other brain was at the wheel. For now, all I could focus on was her bee-stung lips soon to be wrapped around my dick.

CHAPTER TWO

KELLI

Holden handed me a lukewarm dish he'd made from the packaged meals stashed in with the supplies. The tap inside the sanctuary never reached anywhere near hot, so the dehydrated "beef stew" didn't stand a chance at tasting like anything other than the paper it was wrapped in. Still, it was better than the uncertainty of whether I would be fed at all. The running water and a toilet was reason enough to be grateful.

"What flavor is this supposed to be?" I asked, swishing the cloudy drink he gave me.

"The wrapper said Lemonade, but it tastes more like aspartame to me."

"The orange one wasn't awful." I sniffed the pale-yellow drink, trying not to notice how it resembled piss.

Holden nodded as he forked some of his sad-looking stew into his mouth.

This was the sort of brief conversation we'd been having. We hadn't spoken much beyond necessity. Holden kept to himself and constantly walked back and forth in the upstairs rafters, looking through the cracks in the boarded-up windows to scan for signs of danger. Meanwhile, I was sequestered to stay inside one row of pews. On the floor, head hidden. Just in case.

The first night, I was frozen in fear on the floor. Every creak of the floorboards, every owl screeching outside sent me into a panic. The second night, I slept on one of the pews. They didn't have cushions, but it was warmer than the floor. We were on our fifth day here and had settled into a pattern.

We had two meals a day to make the rations last as long as possible. The mornings were spent taking turns in the bathroom. The single bar of soap we shared to wash with was holding strong for now. The stash of items under the floorboards held a small number of toiletries, but if we stayed here much longer, we'd run out of what little luxuries we had. Hell, we'd run out of food soon if nothing changed. Every time I tried to ask about a plan, I was met with a grunt. Either he had no plan or he wasn't willing to trust me with it. My money was on the latter.

Holden kept his position at the upper level most of the day to keep watch, only coming down to check the doors, give me medicine for my finger, or deliver food. While I wasn't in a cage, the cold shoulder and lack of answers started to feel quite similar to when I was trapped by Connor.

"How's the hand?" Holden asked. His grip rested on the gun in his holster. It was always at his side.

"It's fine. Thanks. The splint you made is helping with the throbbing for sure." It wasn't medical grade by any stretch, but the bits of wood and duct tape seemed to help. I wondered if I might be able to keep the finger after all.

"The penicillin should help with anything funky that might try to latch on, and the Oxi should keep the pain at bay but still, these aren't the ideal conditions for healing a wound as traumatic as a severed finger. The supplies here were meant to help with things like gun wounds or gashes. It's not exactly an ER, which is probably where I should have taken you from day one."

I couldn't help but smile.

"What?" he asked.

"Nothing. It's just, that's the longest stretch of words you've said to me in days."

Holden frowned. His massive body deflated for a fraction of a second, letting me know my words upset him. "Sorry. I'm not very good with small talk."

"Isn't that part of the gig? Pretending to be someone else?" I raised a brow. "Surely your undercover self must talk."

"Hired thugs aren't paid for their conversational skills."

I frowned. "Yeah, but you must talk sometime."

"I do. When needed. But that's easy. I'm playing a part then. It's not me talking. It's a character I made up. This guy," he said, gesturing to himself, "he ain't got that much to say."

"I get it. It's nice hearing someone else's voice, though. Well, someone who isn't screaming in agony in a cage beside me, that is. I've heard enough of that to last a lifetime."

Holden was quiet, as if trying to choose the right words. "How long were you there?" A tinge of pity laced his tone.

I tried to recall. "What month is it?"

"September. Don't ask me what day, though. I've lost track of that myself."

September? I did the mental math twice, refusing to believe it had been that long.

"He took me April first. I should have known better to look at apartments on April Fool's Day."

Holden cocked his head. "Five months? That bastard had you locked up for five months?"

I stared at the empty nail bed on my better hand. Connor had torn it off when he'd discovered I'd been using it to mark the walls to count the days.

"Guess so. I thought it was closer to three months. Though, I suppose it does take time to starve someone to the size the client wants. Before all this I actually had boobs, if you can believe it," I said, glancing at what was left of my breasts. "That and another buyer fell through, so there was a lapse. Even still, I would have sworn it was only two and a half months. Three tops. Five is... a lot."

"I can't believe no one came looking for you in that time."

I let slip a soft laugh. "You don't get it. That's his whole thing. Connor screens his applicants, searching for the loners. Those new to town or people with no family or friends. I was both. He hit the lottery with my rental application."

"No family? No boyfriend?" His voice lifted at the end, almost as though he were hopeful I'd say no. "Or girlfriend. Sorry. I shouldn't assume."

That earned him a smile. "No. No family. No *boy*friend. I wish I liked women. Would make my life a lot easier. But even if there was someone, they'd never think I was part of a human trafficking ring."

"But what about work? Someone would have noticed you weren't there?"

"There again, I fit Connor's criteria. I was new to the area. I was a nanny, so I was searching for work since my last family in Oregon had kids that aged out of needing care. Thought I'd have better luck in the city." I shrugged. "He told me he and his wife were looking for a nanny. Maybe the unit tour could double as a job interview. I fell for his lies because I was so desperate to find work. I should have trusted my gut."

"That doesn't make this your fault. You know that, right? Connor is a master manipulator. This isn't on you."

"No, I know. I just shouldn't have let myself trust a man. Burns me every time. Lesson learned." I held up my splinted hand as evidence.

"Kelli, you can trust me. Cop, remember?"

"You say that like it isn't an oxymoron. Some of Connor's men are cops, too, are they not?"

Holden huffed but didn't refute me. But my comment ended the conversation as he went to check the doors again. Guess the truth was a little too much for him to hear. But I wasn't going to sugarcoat things. Not after all I'd lived through. I looked down at my body, sat uncomfortably on the hard pew, and lifted my spoon to eat cold stew. As miserable as I was, I would survive. It was the only thing I knew how to do.

HOLDEN

As much as I hated to admit it, Kelli was right. Cops couldn't be trusted. Especially here. That's part of why I was on such high alert in a place that was supposed to be a safe haven for me. For all I knew, Connor might already be on the way to take us down. There wasn't enough firepower here if he, or his men, attacked. I had about ten rounds on the weapon at my hip, a second Glock stored under the floorboards, and a half dozen magazines. That would be nothing against what Connor might bring. We were sitting ducks, and what was worse... I had no idea who our enemy was.

That was why I had to lie to Kelli about how long we'd have to hide out earlier. The Feds weren't coming in two weeks. While this place was set up for stakeouts, no one in the district knew where I was. And if we wanted to stay alive, we needed proof that would get us to the top of the food chain, where the corruption would be harder to breach. So, I made the only play I had. I knew who Malcolm was. His black-market art trades were on our radar, but he was slippery. Covered his tracks well. So far, there was nothing to pin on him. But he was spotted at Connor's. With the redhead. The redhead I knew was Vincent's final leverage on Connor. If Malcolm saved Amanda from that hell hole, then he must have some clue of what was going on inside. He was a witness. As was Amanda. If I could get either of them to testify...

I knew his address from our files. A location I knew well. I grew up nearby, so I made a risky choice after taking Kelli from Carlos. While we were in the cab, I placed a call to a courier.

I gave Malcolm a time and a place and prayed that someone would find it with all of the security cameras on his property. I knew he'd left the premises, but my only shot of reaching Malcolm and Amanda was that single play. I could only hope Connor's men weren't watching too. It was a major risk to leave the address of where we were, but it wasn't like we could go to them. I had no idea where Malcolm had landed. I had to trust that his team would find the message before Connor's men did.

"Holden?" Kelli's voice from behind me brought me out of my thoughts.

"What is it? Is something wrong?" My eyes darted down to her hand, half expecting it to be oozing puss or turning black. I was no doctor and had no idea if what I had done for her injury would help or hurt. Her hand, however, appeared fine.

"I was just wondering if there were any blankets or anything warm under those floorboards. It gets pretty chilly down here at night."

While it was still summer, the weather was starting its shift into autumn with brisker nights and shorter hours of daylight. I glanced at the oversized T-shirt she had on. It was the only clothing Connor had given her. Of course she'd be cold.

"No blankets, but why don't you sleep upstairs tonight? It's a hell of a lot warmer up there. I'll look around and see if I can find anything that might work as a blanket. In the meantime, you can wear this." I shrugged free of the button-up shirt I was wearing, leaving me in my white tank top and black jeans. The cold didn't bother me. I ran hot. Handing her the shirt, I felt like an ass for not offering it sooner.

"Thanks." She took the shirt and slipped it on. It enveloped her. She hugged the fabric against her skin. "Mmm. It smells like you."

"Oh. Sorry."

"No. That's a good thing. You smell nice."

"Um... thanks?"

Kelli approached me then, her eyes intent on something. "What's the tattoo of?"

A moment later, her fingers were tracing the marks just above where my tank stopped. The heat of her fingers on my skin had me retreating backward, as though I'd been shot.

"Sorry," she whispered.

"No. It's fine. I'm just... not used to people touching me." I turned away and checked the doors again. I needed the distraction.

"Got it. No small talk. No human contact," Kelli said. "Just sit down, shut up, and do as you're told." Her voice deflated. Guilt washed over me. The poor woman must be so deprived of human kindness and simple conversation after what she'd been through. And here I was barely talking to her and treating her like a problem I needed to solve.

My shoulders slumped. I sat across the aisle in the opposite one she was sitting in. "I'm sorry. I guess I've forgotten how to talk to people. I've been undercover for nearly a year now. The company I kept wasn't exactly what you'd call polite society. You learn pretty fast to keep your mouth shut and speak only when spoken to."

"Not unlike Connor's training," Kelli said, pushing a mushy carrot around her bowl with the plastic spoon.

"Do you want to talk about it?"

She shook her head. "No. I want to know about what is under your shirt. Is it a tattoo? A scar?"

I stood up. "I mean no offense, but I don't want to talk about it. I won't press you on your time with Connor, and you don't press me on this," I said, touching the spot she was curious about. "Now finish your dinner so we can get you upstairs. We'll lose the sun soon."

"We all have secrets, Holden. It's okay. You don't have to tell me yours. I sure as shit aren't telling you mine." She seemed to force herself to eat the last bites of her food before she grabbed her drink to follow me to the second floor.

Part of me was relieved she hadn't pressed me on the issue. The other part of me was dying to let it out. Maybe then it wouldn't have such a hold on my psyche. She'd been through insane trauma. She might understand... I shook my head. No. She had enough to deal with. This was my cross to bear.

CHAPTER THREE

AMANDA

Watching Malcolm's head roll back as I sucked his cock, I knew he was lost in the feeling of my lips against him. Which is exactly what I wanted. I needed him to be weak in the knees. Unsuspecting. He was hiding something from me. And whatever it was, it was in his back pocket. I could see the edge of the paper sticking out. He had quickly shoved the paper into his pants, hoping I'd been too zoned out to notice when we stopped earlier in the day.

Before our final stop at the house, Malcolm had the cab pull over at some coffee shop to make a call. He'd stepped outside to do it, which was what made it odd. Did he not want me to hear something? Or maybe he was making sure the driver didn't overhear?

Through the window, I watched as he called someone. I had to assume it was either Camilla or Darcy. His face darkened as he spoke to them. Realizing he was showing emotion, he turned his back to the cab and then went inside the coffee shop, obscuring my view. That was not like Malcolm. He wouldn't just leave me alone with a stranger.

A moment later, Malcolm came out of the shop. His cell phone was gone, probably trashed inside. He went into the cab, where I pretended to be asleep. Whatever that call was about, or what was in his pocket, he hadn't felt the need to share it with me, which could only mean that it was bad news. News I was going to uncover, whether he wanted me to or not.

And now, with his dick in my mouth and his pants on the floor beside his feet, my answer was mere inches from my grasp.

"Fuck, Amanda, you're amazing." Malcolm's hands dug into my hair, positioning my head at the angle he needed. Taking this moment of his unbalance, I pushed his dick out of my mouth, making him stumble backward. I scrambled free of the tub, grabbed his pants, and beelined it to the bedroom door. I slammed it shut and shoved my body against it.

"Amanda! What are you doing?" Malcolm called from the bathroom.

I took a few seconds to catch my breath. "You're hiding something from me."

"I'm what? Amanda, what are you talking about?"

"What's this note in your back pocket?"

The silence from the other side of the door was all the evidence I needed.

"I can explain," he said after a moment.

"Men always can." I took the pants, grabbed the paper, and opened it. It was a handwritten note on what looked like a discarded napkin. It was Malcolm's handwriting. I scanned the message.

"Gwen is safe. Need to talk. Bring A," I whispered the words aloud, hardly able to process them. My mind went instantly to Connor, but the message seemed to be signed by someone named "H."

Thoroughly confused, I opened the bathroom door, holding the proof in my hand. "Who the hell is H?"

Malcolm let out a deep sigh. He looked rather deflated standing in just his button-down shirt with no pants.

"I was going to tell you. Tomorrow. Once we both got some rest. I promise."

I shoved the note at his chest. "I'll ask again, who the hell is H?"

"I don't know. Seriously. A courier showed up and left it at the house the day of the fire. Camila had one of our men collect it. I don't know what any of it means."

"That address. Where is it? Is it local?"

Malcolm pinched his fingers to his brow. "According to GPS, it's an abandoned church. Photos of the place show 'no trespassing' signs everywhere. Warnings of asbestos abatement. Just the sort of place Connor would use as a hideout."

"But it's not Connor. It's some guy named H."

"Amanda, that could be a ruse. Or the name of one of his goons."

I shook my head. "But if he has Kelli—"

Confusion washed over Malcolm's face. "Oh right. Gwen is the name they gave Kelli for her new master. I forgot. Even so, if they have Kelli that doesn't involve us."

"Like hell, it doesn't. If Kelli is being held hostage, we need to try and help her."

Malcolm put his arms over my shoulders and walked me to the bed. He was trying to soothe my anxiety, but there was no coming down from this.

"Look, I know you want to help your friend, but this isn't a rescue situation. It's a bait and switch. They want to lure you in with the promise of saving your friend, only to take you out in the process. It's a trap, Amanda. An obvious one."

I nodded. "Agreed. Which is why I don't think Connor is involved. He would never be so careless. I think this might be legit." That's when the memory hit me. "H! I know who that is! It's Holden! His name is Holden!"

Malcolm froze. "What? How do you know that?"

"He was one of the two men transferring Kelli. I could hear them out in the hall on the day of the fire. Holden was a new guy. Connor didn't trust him. Malcolm, *Connor didn't trust him*! That must mean that Holden isn't working with Connor. Maybe he saved Kelli before the fire started." A surge of hope welled inside of me. Kelli might be alive. Safe.

"Amanda, that doesn't mean anything. Aren't you forgetting the last sentence of that message? 'Bring A.' That's you. If this Holden guy is so innocent, and just being chivalrous, what the fuck does he want with you?"

I bit my lip. "I don't know. But that's what we're going to find out. I'm going to that church, Malcolm. You can come with me or not, but I'm going to see if Kelli is there. I have failed her too many times. She's sacrificed so much for me. I owe her this."

His eyes darkened. "You're not going to risk your life on what is clearly a setup. Think rationally for a second."

"Rational? You want me to think rationally after everything I've been through? Everything has been irrational since the day I walked into Connor's building." I was shouting, and I knew that it only made me appear hysterical, so I let free a steadying breath, squared my shoulders, and then tried again. "Look, I know you think this is a trap. And maybe it is. But we're smart. Or, rather, you are. You'll come up with a plan. We can pack as many guns as you want. You can hire snipers to be on rooftops, covering us or some shit. Whatever you need to do to make this meeting work for you, I'm on board with. But I *will* be going to that church. With or without your help."

MALCOLM

I knew that look on Amanda's face. She was determined. She really would go to the address with just her plucky attitude, thinking she could take on whatever was behind those doors alone. I had to cool her off and either convince her that was the worst idea ever, or more than likely, devise a safe way to investigate the place without getting killed in the process.

Grabbing my pants back, I slid them on. "Okay. Let's come up with a plan. Step one: research," I said, walking through the living room to a large painting of mine on the wall. I placed my thumb on the fingerprint sensor under the frame. It unlocked the hidden panel. Swinging it open, I watched as my display of monitors and CPUs appeared in full view.

"Jesus. Are you a spy?" Amanda asked, walking over beside me.

"No. Just more paranoid than the average person." I keyed in my password, and the screens came to life. "Okay, first things first, let's do a search of the property itself. I want to scour the internet for more pictures. Find the entrances and exits. Possible places Connor's goons might be hiding out nearby. That sort of thing."

She crossed her arms over her chest. "How long will that take?"

"Depends on what my search finds, but this isn't a five-minute plan. It could take hours or days."

"Days?" She gasped.

"Yes. *If* we go, we're going to make sure we have the safest way in."

"Kelli might be dead in that time. And the note mentioned a specific time to come."

I turned around and frowned at her. "And I'm ignoring his demand. Look, if we do this it needs to be on my terms. And don't worry about Kelli. He's not going to kill his only bargaining chip. Whether that is this Holden guy or if it's Connor. If Kelli is the bait, whoever has her will keep her alive until they get what they want. Which seems to be you." My fingers went back to their assault on the keyboard.

Behind me, Amanda watched as I worked for a few minutes before she huffed. "Fine. I suppose your idea has merit. While you do your hacker thing, I'm going to take a shower and maybe find us some food."

"Solid plan," I said as my eyes scanned the pages coming up on my screen. A moment later, I felt her lips hit the top of my head.

"Thank you, Malcolm. You're always looking out for me. Reminding me that I don't have to do stuff alone. I'm not used to that."

"I'm not used to wanting to help someone other than myself," I added. "So, thank you for teaching me selflessness."

She gave me a genuine smile. "Look at us... being mentally stable adults."

I laughed as she padded off to her shower. I wasn't sure what data I'd be able to pull up on the situation given the limited details of the information, but I was going to do my darndest to talk her out of this insane plan.

A few hours later, I wasn't much further than when I started. Amanda had scrounged around in the kitchen to make spaghetti with ingredients I didn't even know I had, and we feasted at the dining room table as I broke down what little I'd discovered.

"For starters, the asbestos abatement is a ruse," I said, swirling the pasta around my fork. "A ploy to keep people out."

"How do you know that?"

"Because the building was built in 1991," I said, as though that explanation should be obvious.

"I don't follow. Why does when it was built matter?" A bit of sauce dribbled on her chin. I wanted to reach over and lick it off, but she wiped it away before I could.

"They banned asbestos in 1990, so the sign is an outright lie that it's present. Second, a church that new shouldn't be so dilapidated. And yet, even though it seems abandoned..." I tilted the screen toward her so she could see what I was noticing. "Look at the front doors."

I watched as Amanda took in the tall red arched doors at the front of the sanctuary. She shrugged her shoulders.

"They look like pretty standard church doors to me," she said.

I zoomed in on the image. "What about those locks? Those look a tad too modern for an abandoned building, wouldn't you say? I wouldn't be surprised if they were fingerprint scan locks like

I have. Why would a deserted church need that much security? And the location... That's another red flag."

"What's wrong with the location? Where even is Woods Creek? Is that in the state?"

"It's about forty-five minutes from here."

"Ok... so why is that a red flag?" Amanda took a bite of her pasta.

"Think about it. If you're the bad guy, and you have Kelli, why would you bring her to Woods Creek? Why not get as far away from the scene of the crime as you can?" I rubbed my forehead, trying to make some logical conclusions to it all.

"Hmm. What's the play then? Can you send some of your guys out there to sniff around? See if they can find anything?"

"My guys?"

"Yeah. You know. Have them scope out the place. See if it seems fishy."

I cocked my head. "Amanda, I'm not Connor. I don't have hired thugs at my beck and call ready to put their life on the line for me. I have Darcy and Camilla. That's it. And I want them in deep hiding right now. I'm not pulling them in any more than I have to."

"Right. I'm sorry. I just assumed with all this money—"

"That I'd have no regard for human life?"

Amanda shrugged. "That *has* been my experience as of late."

I reached across the table and took her hand. She seemed startled at the gesture but relaxed when she realized I wasn't trying to hurt her.

"We'll find Kelli. The cops will find Connor. Then this nightmare will be over. I promise."

She didn't need to say anything, but I could already tell she had no faith in my vow. I had no way of ensuring the delivery of any of it. And she and I both knew it.

CHAPTER FOUR

KELLI

Holden was right. The loft was warmer but had the same amount of disarray as the lower level: torn red carpet and boarded-up stained-glass windows. It didn't have pews as downstairs did, but rather, wooden movie-style seating where the chair popped up when not in use. There would be no comfortable way to lay across them, given the way the armrests connected. Great.

"You shouldn't blame yourself, you know," Holden said.

I glanced at him as he watched for signs of danger through a crack in the boards.

"Blame myself for what? Being stupid enough to trust an ad in the paper?"

He turned to look at me. "For any of it. These men who run these rings... They know what they're doing. They know how to manipulate people. They are vultures. And they're very good at hunting the perfect candidate. Once they have you in their sights, it's almost impossible to escape the traps they lay. I've seen it. Over and over again."

"Do any of the women go free? Those that you've seen get taken?"

Holden lowered his head. "Not a one. Some die at the hands of their new masters or come back for disobeying. Vincent doesn't bother to retrain. He just puts them out of their misery."

"Jesus." I shivered. "Have you... Have you ever had to do that? Put someone out of their misery?"

"No. Thank God. Vincent likes to do that work himself. I think that's his kink, honestly. Ultimate punishment. I swear sometimes he doesn't train the girls at all so he can have the satisfaction of killing them later when they ultimately get returned."

"Would you, though? Kill one of the women? If Vincent ordered you to?"

Holden's eyebrows pulled tight as he stood tall. "Absolutely not. The day he asked would be the day I broke cover. Guess I don't need to worry about my cover now. My head will be as high on the hit list as yours. You don't steal from men like this and live to tell about it."

"Yeah, that was pretty stupid of you."

That earned me a rare smile. It made my stomach flutter at how soft it made his face.

"It was stupid. But it's also something I should have done a hell of a lot sooner. The nightmares I have at night about all the women I've seen taken, abused, and sold off like cattle while undercover... It just makes it hard to trust that anything I've done will end it. The evidence I'm gathering, will it even matter, knowing how corrupt so many cops are? Or how tightly these monsters protect their paper trails? Will any of this be worth it?" He scrubbed his hand over his face.

It took everything in me not to pull him into a hug he desperately needed.

"You should get some rest," he said. "I'll keep watch."

That was my signal to shut up. He wasn't going to give me any more tonight. I wasn't overly tired, but there wasn't much else to do, so I decided to appease him. Sighing, I made my way to the floor, since sleeping in the chairs would be pointless.

As I was lowering my body to the ground, I froze mid-crouch.

My eyes locked on to where the balcony seats were bolted to the floor. *Bolted furniture. Just like in Connor's cages.* The physical reaction came out of nowhere as my body catapulted itself away from the chairs so fast, I nearly fell on my ass.

"Whoa, you okay?" Holden asked as he grabbed onto my waist to steady me.

I shook my head and tried to push out of his grasp, but he held me tighter, eventually pulling me into his chest as my breathing grew more frantic.

"Hey, hey. It's okay. You're okay."

I tried to move again, but his soft whispers calmed me in a way I didn't think possible.

"Shh, it's okay. I've got you. You're safe."

It took several rounds of him repeating those words until I was able to slow my breathing. I let him hold me for a few more moments because I didn't want to open my eyes to reality. I wanted to stay in this warm cocoon of his embrace and believe his words. That I was okay. That I was safe.

Eventually, I pulled myself together, and he released me from his arms. I straightened up but still took two large steps away from the chairs.

"Sorry."

"No need to apologize. What happened? What spooked you?"

"It's stupid," I said, tears pricking my eyes. I pointed to the chairs. "I saw that they were bolted to the floor and... I don't know. I panicked. It reminded me of the furniture in my cage."

Holden looked at me and then glanced at the chairs. "He bolted the furniture down?"

"That way we couldn't use them as weapons against him," I said. "He was brilliant in his cruelty. He gave us nothing that could harm him—or ourselves. One girl hung herself with a bedsheet. Guess what we all lost the privilege of the next day?" I kicked at a spot on the ground.

"Jesus," Holden whispered. "I knew the guy was a monster, but that's a new level of twisted."

"Connor runs a human sex slave operation. Twisted is just the tip of how fucked up he is. Exhibit A." I held up my finger. "This is what you get when someone else tries to run away."

"We'll find him, Kelli. The authorities will make him pay for what he did to you. For what he's done to all of them."

"What about the women who didn't get out? I know there was at least one other in that building when it burned. Belinda. She didn't speak English." My voice cracked. "And who knows how many others were on the floors below us?"

"Do you know how many he kept on your floor?"

I shook my head.

"I only knew the people on either side of me. Belinda on the right. Amanda to my left." My eyes widened. "Amanda! She was with Connor in her cage when you took me. Did he... Is she?"

"We think she got out. No remains were found in her room. Vincent's goons observed a 'Malcolm Luxx' on a traffic camera exiting the parking garage of Connor's moments before the fire department arrived. We believe Amanda might be with him."

I gave Holden an odd look. "Who is Malcolm Luxx? One of Connor's men?"

He seemed to hedge before he spoke. "Vincent seems to think Malcolm was a buyer but ran once the fire broke out."

"But you don't think that's what happened?" I watched his face carefully. He seemed to be calculating his thoughts.

"I don't know anything for sure. For all I know, he could have kidnapped Amanda to use as leverage against Connor... but my gut tells me he was rescuing her."

"I'm not sure I follow your logic." I might have spent time in a cage, but I didn't have the mind of these criminals.

"If Malcolm had taken one of Connor's pets for revenge or to brag or whatever, there would have been sightings of him with her. Proof to rub it in. That's how these guys operate. It's all about turf wars and marking their territory."

"Well, if he bought her, he could also be hiding because he's afraid to be caught. Buying another human being is still highly illegal, is it not?"

Holden rubbed his face. "It is. I just don't think that's what happened. Maybe it's wishful thinking. I don't want to believe Malcolm is one of the bad guys."

"In my experience, men always are." I regretted it as soon as I saw Holden's face drop. Without meaning to, I'd lumped him into the same category as Connor. "Sorry. That was unfair to you."

"You don't need to apologize. I tend to agree with you." Holden glanced at the darkening church below. "You forget the company I've kept recently." He gave me a small smile. "You should get some sleep."

"What about you? Don't you need sleep?"

He shrugged. "I'm used to little to no sleep. Kinda the gig."

"That's not healthy."

"Neither is letting Connor roam the earth."

Holden went to one of the lookouts near the window while I found a spot against the wall with no chairs. The floor was hard and cold and dirty as hell, but as weary as my bones felt, I was glad for the chance to rest. I fell asleep faster than I would have thought.

At some point during the night, I heard a noise and woke up. For a moment, I was in full panic until I got my bearings. Then, I heard the noise again. A whisper. From Holden. I couldn't make out what he said because it was so soft, but my eyes darted to him, expecting to see him signaling me to some danger. But his eyes were closed. He was leaning against the doors that led downstairs. Literally using his body as a shield. His gun was at his side. Inches away from use should the occasion arise.

"Shannon," he mumbled. This time his voice was loud enough to hear. In the moonlight, I could see that his eyes were moving rapidly behind his lids. He was dreaming. Of a woman named Shannon. Why that made me irrationally jealous, I couldn't say.

"Stop. Don't go," he said. "Shannon. Please. I'll make it better. Give me time." His voice was growing more frantic now. Furrowed brows and elevated breathing told me his dream was far from pleasant. Being left never was.

An overwhelming sense of compassion washed over me as I moved my body a few feet toward him. As his breathing intensified, I rested a hand on his thigh to try to soothe him. A moment later, so quickly that I didn't even know how it happened, he pulled me onto his lap and held me tightly against his chest. "Shannon. Thank God. You came back."

I sat there, frozen in his arms as he held me. I couldn't have squirmed out if I wanted to. And I didn't want to. Even though he was dreaming about another woman, I couldn't deny the feeling of being held like this. The comfort that there were men in the world who loved their women so fiercely they would not want to let them go. It almost made me believe that love might be real for some people.

Almost.

HOLDEN

When I awoke in the morning, Kelli was in my arms. How and when did Kelli get in my arms? And why was I not already moving her off me? I supposed it was partly because she looked so peaceful with her head rising and falling on my chest with the sounds of my breathing. Her fingers had curled themselves into my shirt, as though clinging onto something safe. Not that I could blame her.

After the time she'd spent being a captive, I didn't want to deny her a feeling of safety, if only in slumber. It was, however, inconvenient how much I liked the way she felt in my arms. But that was probably the lack of female companionship as of late than any true feelings. I didn't do feelings. Or relationships. They only got in the way of my work.

The twitch in my cock was only because her body was pressed against mine. Basic human instinct. That was all.

Just then, Kelli stirred. I released my unintended grip on her and held my hands in the air so when she did wake, she wouldn't think I was trying anything funny. She had climbed into my arms, after all. If anyone had some explaining to do, it was her.

"Mmm." The soft moans that escaped her lips as she started to wake up were not helping the semi I was sporting. The grip she had on my shirt released as she moved her hands instead to around my torso in a deep embrace. Followed by another soft moan. Cue a full erection.

That was when she lifted her eyelids. She looked up at me, as though registering where she was, then she quickly pushed herself off me. Her eyes darted down at my obvious arousal. "Is that a... Are you hard?"

I groaned and stood up. I holstered my gun and headed to the opposite side of the church.

"Morning wood. Happens to guys all the time. Don't flatter yourself."

"Flatter myself?" I heard her repeat.

I willed my cock to shrink. He wasn't listening.

"I mean, I don't want you to think you had something to do with this situation. It's just a thing that men have to deal with, okay?"

"Is that your polite way of saying you don't find me attractive?" Kelli laughed. She didn't seem bothered by that possible reality, but I hated that it was her assumption.

"I didn't say that. I'm trying to clarify that just because you tucked yourself against me in the night for warmth or whatever, that doesn't mean—"

"Wait. You think *I* cuddled *you*?" I turned around to look at her, my cock finally relaxing. Her eyes were ablaze. "I didn't cuddle you, asshole," she continued. "You were having a bad dream. I rested a hand on you to try and calm you, and then, *you* pulled me into your arms before locking me in place with your freakishly large biceps."

"I pulled you to me?" I asked, not remembering a single moment of that.

Kelli nodded, then stared at the ground. "Just before you called me Shannon."

Hearing that name aloud nearly brought me to my knees. The pain flooded over me, clouding my vision.

"Who is Shannon?" Kelli asked, but I didn't respond. Instead, I turned on my heel and left her in the loft while I went downstairs to check the perimeter. That was one name that was never meant to be uttered in mixed company. And here I had said it in my sleep? That was reckless. Stupid. And I was not stupid. Or at least I hadn't been up until recently.

Since meeting Kelli, I'd done one reckless thing after another. I didn't even have a logical reason for putting my neck on the line for her. I should have done what I'd done countless times before. Make the transport, then report as much info about the drop as I could in the hopes that they would be found later. My mission was to stay undercover, gather the evidence on the ring so they could take the whole thing down. My mission was not to save one for the sake of the rest. I still don't know why I reacted that way. It was instinctual. I had to save Kelli. And for some reason, I couldn't bring myself to regret my choice.

CHAPTER FIVE

AMANDA

When I woke the next morning, my fingers instinctively reached across the bed to find Malcolm. Yet, instead of finding his warm chest, I discovered nothing but cold sheets. Cracking an eye open, I noticed he wasn't beside me. I fought against the panic of why he might be missing but assured myself that no one knew we were living in a hidden space under Malcolm's couch. Connor couldn't have found us, let alone managed to get Malcolm out of bed without me hearing anything.

Glancing at the bathroom, I saw the light was off. *Hmm*. Not in there either. Why wasn't he in bed? Was he angry at me? That could be. I mean, I did betray his trust by sucking him off only as a distraction to discover what he'd been hiding from me. I'd probably be pretty pissed, too, if I'd been used like that.

Sliding free of the covers, I pulled on the T-shirt he'd discarded before he got into bed. His scent enveloped me. My arms wrapped around my body, trying to hold the fabric closer to my skin. That's when I heard Malcolm's voice. He was talking low to someone.

Tiptoeing into the living room, I saw him pacing the floor, talking on one of his many burner phones.

"Yes. That's right. Just survey the area. Pictures of entrances and exits. Anything you can safely get without bringing attention to yourself. Note anything out of the ordinary or if you see any signs of life inside. Do *not* engage or linger. It is imperative that you not be seen as suspicious."

I took another step inside the living room. Malcolm's back was still to me. "Yes," he said into the phone. "Half now, and half when you send me the report." Another moment passed before he hung up. He sighed, shoulders slumping as he did.

"Who was that?"

Malcolm flinched and spun around, eyes widening. "Jesus. You scared the shit out of me."

"Sorry. I woke up, and you weren't in bed so..."

He sucked in a slow breath. "Yeah, well, I couldn't sleep. What you said about Connor—about how he would have hired thugs to scope out the place. It got me thinking. While I don't have hit men on speed dial, I could hire a private detective. Have them do some basic recon. If we're going to go there, I need to be damn sure it's not a trap."

"*If*? Does that mean you are at least considering going now?"

He shrugged. "Only if the report comes back with what I need to hear."

"And how long will this report take?"

"A few days, I imagine. This sort of work takes time. Hiding in plain sight is not as easy as you might think."

I felt myself nod. While I wasn't in love with the idea of waiting, I did understand his caution. It would be wiser to know what we were walking into beforehand. I worried if Kelli could wait that long.

Malcolm walked to the couch and collapsed. He looked exhausted. I went over to him and sat on the ottoman the size of three of me and positioned myself in front of him. Resting my hand on his knee, he cracked an eyelid to look at me.

"Can I get you anything? Coffee? Breakfast?"

"I'm okay. I'm just tired." His body language betrayed him. He appeared to be holding the weight of the world. Because of me.

"Are you sure I can't interest you in something to nibble on?" I lifted my T-shirt to expose my bare left tit. His eyes grew wide. Then hungry.

"You know, I still need payback for what you did to me earlier."

"I agree." I smirked. "Make me pay for being naughty." I spread my legs wide, stretching the bottom of the shirt and exposing myself to him.

"On second thought. I am hungry. Ravenous. And I know just what I want to eat."

With that, he sat up and lowered me down onto the ottoman. He made quick work of taking off the shirt and tossing it aside. His lips met my breast, and I cried out in desire. Fuck, he knew how to turn me on. When he moved to the other breast, I felt his long fingers slide inside me. I gasped at the sensation of his tongue on my nipple and his finger circling me in tandem.

"So wet," he murmured against my breast.

"You keep sucking my tits like this and I'm going to be even wetter." That earned me a gentle bite against my nipple. My hips rose off the ottoman of their own accord to meet his magic fingers.

"You like that, don't you?" He nipped again, and once more my hips rose to meet an unfulfilled need.

"Please, I need you inside me," I begged. Malcolm paused his sucking to lift his head. His eyes met mine. A possessive look came over his face. A look I knew well. I was relinquishing my control. I closed my eyes, preparing myself to be taken. Claimed. Abused. Whatever he wanted to use me for. I was ready to accept it. "Please, Connor."

Malcolm was off me in an instant. "Connor?"

My eyes flicked open as I realized what I'd said. "I... I don't know why I said that." I honestly didn't.

"I do." Malcolm took several steps away. "It means you still care for him. Or worse, you're still so sexually traumatized that you went into survival mode. Either way, one thing is clear. You are not ready to have sex. Least of all with me." His slumped shoulders seemed to go even lower. "I'm going to take a shower. Please don't join me. I need to be alone right now."

He retreated into the bathroom, and as much as I wanted to follow him and tell him that he was wrong. That Connor's name was just a slip of the tongue, I couldn't. Because what if he was right? No. I didn't have feelings for Connor. The man terrified me. Unless he was filling me, then he gave me the best sex of my life. Which in and of itself was insanity. But Malcolm also had another point. Was this trauma? The second I anticipated sex with a man who could overpower me... who could hurt me... I closed my eyes and prepared myself for the assault. *Assault.* I was preparing to be hurt.

Fuck.

MALCOLM

One sure way to calm an erection? Have the woman you loved call you another man's name. But to say *that* name... It was too much to process. I didn't love either of my theories as to why she might have said it. Because both answers meant she didn't love me. And why would she? A recluse loner with poor social habits. What could I possibly offer her, other than my wealth?

When I got out of the shower, Amanda was sitting on the bed. She'd put on another one of my T-shirts. It swam on her as she sat cross-legged. Her head was bowed low. Submissive. Probably like she'd been trained to do when she had upset her "Master."

"Amanda, lift your head. You're not some dog who misbehaved. I'm not going to punish you for what you said."

"You should." She sniffed. "I deserve it."

My heart sank, knowing she honestly believed that. I walked over to the bed and knelt on the floor so I could find her eyes. "Hey, Amanda. Listen to me. I'm not going to hurt you. Nothing you do or say is going to cause me to raise a hand against you."

She lifted her head. Her eyebrows pinched together. "Why not? I deserve it! I said another man's name as we were about to have sex. That should earn me at least a smack across the face. A belt to the ass. Choking me until I pass out. Something. I deserve something other than your fucking compassion. I did an awful, unforgivable thing. Why won't you punish me for it?"

The tears streamed down her face. She was upset with me. For *not* hurting her. How fucked up was that?

"You didn't do anything to warrant physical abuse, Amanda. *Nothing* you could ever do would. I know that's a foreign concept for you, and that it hasn't been your lived experience, but don't forget my mother died at the hands of her abuser. The last thing I would ever want to do is hurt a woman. Let alone you."

Her bottom lip quivered as she absorbed my words. I could tell she was trying her best to believe them. She came to me then and wrapped her arms around me. I pulled her in tight to me as she sobbed softly against my chest. I held her for several minutes until her breath finally returned to normal.

"Thank you," she whispered. "Thank you for always reminding me that I am worth more than I think I am."

"I'll remind you every day if you need it."

She lifted her head off my chest. Her eyes were still red, but the tears had stopped. "Don't make promises you can't keep." Pushing away from me, she went out into the living room. Confused, I followed her, still in my towel from the shower.

"Amanda... did I upset you just now?"

Her eyes were vacant, lost to some thought I wasn't included in. She curled her legs up to her chest, then wrapped her arms around herself, as though she were trying to appear as small as possible. She was going through something in her mind. Something she wasn't ready to talk about. So, I did the only thing I could. I sat beside her and waited.

It took an hour, but eventually, she seemed to come around. She reached out a hand and laced hers with mine. The squeeze she gave my hand sent warmth through my body. Assuring me that I'd done the right thing by sitting with her through whatever it was she'd just gone through.

"Wanna talk about it?" I asked.

"I don't know if I can explain it in a way that will make any sense to you," she whispered.

"Try me."

She let loose a heavy sigh as she leaned her head on my chest. "The first time I had sex was when I was thirteen. I was raped by a guy in our building."

"Jesus."

She shrugged. "I told my dad because I was bleeding after. I was so scared. I hadn't gotten my periods yet, so I thought I might be dying. He didn't do anything about it. Told me to take a shower and stop bleeding everywhere. Then, he yelled at me, saying I shouldn't be walking around in those short shorts. What did I expect would happen?"

"What a dick."

"Yes. But he taught me a valuable lesson that day. No one was going to take care of me, but me. So, I cleaned myself up, tossed the underwear, and made it a point to wear short shorts for as long as I could stand the cold."

My eyes widened. "What? Why?"

"Because fuck them, that's why. I should be able to wear whatever I want. That defiance stayed with me through middle school and high school, as you know. And the way I dressed earned me the type of attention that wasn't remotely healthy, but... it *was* attention." She grew quiet for a moment, then continued, "They might be hitting me or hurting me, but at least they knew I was in the room. More than I can say for my dad. It's twisted, but I started to equate mistreatment as a man's way of loving me. The more they mistreated me, the more they must love me. And Connor... he was the worst at it, which also made him the best in a sick way. Deep down, I think I convinced myself that I could change him. That all he needed was the love of a good woman. After all, that's what I thought would fix me. Someone to love me. I was delusional. Love doesn't fix shit."

"Give me some time. There is a lot to fix, with both of us," I said with a smile, kissing the top of her head gently.

She squeezed my hand. "I really am sorry for saying his name. You might be right. I might need some therapy to work through the trauma. Maybe ignoring what I've been through isn't the healthiest path."

"I can set up something as soon as tomorrow."

She shook her head. "No. Not until Kelli is safe."

I scowled but nodded. "Okay. Deal."

Moving herself off me, she patted my knee. "Are we okay?"

"We are." I smiled. I was thrilled she was finally opening up to me about her past. The pieces were clicking into place: how sex and love got so messed up in her mind.

Letting go of my knee, she stood up. "It's my turn to take a shower." Her long legs stepped over mine. "I know you won't join me. But you're welcome to."

I hated that my cock twitched at the invitation. "I don't think that's wise. You need time to process. Heal."

"I didn't say we'd have sex. I said you could watch me."

Frowning, I tilted my head to the side. "Because watching you shower isn't going to get me hard?"

She gave me a wicked smile. "I would be offended if it didn't. But so what? Are you saying that because of what I told you, we aren't allowed to mess around or get ourselves off? Are we meant to be celibate now?"

"No. Amanda, of course that's not what I'm saying—"

With that, she lifted her shirt, exposing her perfect body to me. Cue the hard-on. "Good. I'll be in the shower then. Join me or don't. Your choice." She cupped her breasts, and I let out an involuntary moan. Squeezing both her nipples, she smirked and then headed for the shower.

I lasted a grand total of two and a half seconds before my ass was off the couch and following her to the bathroom. So much for my morals.

CHAPTER SIX

CONNOR

Shelter update: Pet "A" is still missing—crews are out hunting. Pets "B" and "P" crossed the rainbow bridge. The rest are accounted for and in new cages. Pet "K" spotted. Rescue is scouting the area for signs of her and her handler. Will update you when there's more.

I ground my teeth together, looking at Carlos's text. Of all the pets he'd accounted for after the fire, Amanda's whereabouts was what most concerned me. On the one hand, I was relieved she'd made it out of the fire. On the other, I was livid it was Malcolm who had rescued her. It had to be. According to my ear on the inside of the police station, only two dead bodies were recovered from the fire. Belinda and Patricia. Patricia must have tried to go up and save the others and got herself killed in the process. Shame. She gave great head.

If Malcolm had Amanda, he would have taken her to one of his other safehouses. It would take time for me to figure out where they'd run to, but eventually, some camera would spot them. Some digital footprint they didn't realize they'd left would surface, and then, I would have my answers. For now, I had bigger fish to fry. My Seattle shelter was lost, and I still had owners awaiting their pets' deliveries. As time was short, I'd have to tap into the inventory at my Canadian kennel. Bringing pets over the border was a hassle, but desperate times called for desperate measures.

I'd been hiding out for about a week, and so far, only Carlos had reached out. So far, so good. None of the three-letter bureaus were on to me yet. As such, I risked my first call to Vincent.

"Well, well, well, look who rose from the ashes?" Vincent sang after the fourth ring.

"No thanks to you."

"Me? What did I do?" Vincent asked. His tone was light. The bastard was up to something.

"One of your men burned me: Holden. Meathead-looking kind of dude."

"Ah, Holden. He's a good kid. Loyal. Knows where his bread is buttered," Vincent assured.

I rose and paced the small room I'd carved out for myself in a place that looked, from the outside, to be an abandoned business. Boarded up and in disrepair from the public side, but on the inside, a thriving human trafficking ring hideout.

"Well, your *loyal* thug stole one of my pets." I seethed. "You owe me thirty k for that lost down payment. And I expect you to deliver the stolen pet and bring me this Holden guy so I can blow his brains out for taking what's mine."

Vincent was quiet for a moment before the phone shifted along with his tone. "I ain't paying you shit, Connor. Quite the opposite, in fact."

I stopped mid-pace. *What was he talking about?*

"The way I see it," Vincent went on, "I did you a favor."

"A favor? What favor was that?" My eyebrows pinched together as I tried to figure out what his angle was.

"That thug of mine, as you like to call him? Did you know that he's an undercover cop?"

My blood ran cold. Vincent sent an undercover cop to my place of business?

"Bullshit. No way you'd keep a cop in your operation."

Vincent laughed. "Well, the kid was a hard nut to crack. He

played his part well. It took me a while to piece it together, but I eventually got it out of him. See, every man has a weak spot. They all break in the end."

"So, if you knew he was a cop, why did you send him to my business? Why didn't you off him?"

At that, Vincent sucked air through his teeth. "Here I thought you were smarter than that. You ain't figured it out? Holden's real target was *you*. I'm small potatoes and outside U.S. jurisdiction, but you? You're the real prize."

My nostrils flared as I contemplated his reply. Before I could answer, however, he spoke again.

"Now, Holden got me to thinking. Maybe he's onto something. Maybe I should go after you too. So, I say we start the bidding at five hundred k."

My temples throbbed. "Bidding? Bidding on what? I don't need new pets. I have other shelters, asshole. I don't need your strays."

"Oh, I may have one or two you might want." Vincent let out a chuckle, and then I heard it. A man's voice. Muffled. "Hey, Connor? When's the last time you heard from your Pops?"

No. Impossible. He was with Carlos. They were on their way to my Atlanta house.

"See, the thing about *my* men, Connor, is that they are loyal. If I ask them to do something for me, they do it."

"Carlos is *my* man," I snapped.

"All men can be bought. You should know that. Turns out Carlos's price was only a hundred k. Sad, really. Now, as I was saying, five hundred k in exchange for one old drunk. A steal, if you ask me. Or, if you'd rather do a layaway program, I could deliver him a limb at a time, snail mail style?" More muffled screaming.

"If you lay one finger on my father—"

"Oops."

Through the phone, I heard a cry and the unmistakable sizzle of burning flesh. The fucker was branding him with his name. It was his kink—delivering pain. And a branding iron was his weapon of choice. It caused great agony, but not detrimental damage to the property, so they could still be sold off. It was his way of marking his territory even after they'd been sold.

"Pretty pathetic taking advantage of an old man." I tried to hide the emotion in my tone, but I didn't pull it off.

"I could give two shits about him. Don't you get it yet, Connor? I don't *just* want your money. I want your entire empire."

"Why? You have your own empire? Why the hell do you need mine?" I hissed.

Vincent laughed. "You know why. You've been encroaching on my market for far too long. Despite my warning to keep your fishing out of the southern states. We had an arrangement, Connor. You took the North, and I took the South. But you got greedy. Didn't you?"

"We never had any such agreement, you fuck."

"Unspoken agreements are still binding in my book. And according to my logs, in the last seven years alone, you have pulled in fifteen women from Louisiana, Texas, and even Georgia. You know my mama was from Georgia."

My teeth ground together. I did have some vague recollection that his family was from the South before he moved the bulk of his operations across the border where law enforcement was easier to pay off. I never realized how territorial he was.

"Vincent, it's not my fault my clients have twisted slave fetishes. They want the dark, buxom beauties with southern accents. They pay a pretty penny for it."

"I know. Why else do you think we're having this conversation, Fuck Face. You're stealing from *my* pool of kink pets."

"Newsflash, Vincent, you don't own the land women walk on. If I want to source my pets from the South, then I damn well will." Taunting him while he had my father was probably not the smartest play, but his arrogance was pissing me off.

Vincent merely laughed. "Oh, Connor. You still don't get it, do you? You've stolen from me, so I get to steal from you. But I don't just want your women. I'm coming for all your assets. Understand? I'm going to take *everything* of yours."

I couldn't help but laugh. Vincent had been trying to grow beyond his means for years. Not with his ancient bookkeeping skills, let alone how quickly he flew off the handle when things didn't go his way. My business was safe. He was all bark and no bite. An ankle biter at best.

"Good luck with that," I said, ready to hang up.

"Oh, Connor, Connor, Connor. You don't see it yet, do you? How you've already lost. I'm going to bleed you dry, one asset at a time. First your father, then I'll be claiming your previously sold pets. Hell, I'm even going after your loose pets. That certain redhead you've grown attached to? You don't think you're the only one hunting her down, do you?"

I stopped cold.

"How much is she going to be worth to you, Connor? Amanda... that's her name, right? Yeah, I know all about her. Carlos tells me no one is to lay a finger on her. He tells me that you get oddly possessive when you're near her. Wonder why that is? It couldn't be because you've fallen for her, could it?" Vincent's laugh through the phone made me want to punch him in the nuts. "You of all people broke the cardinal rule. Never fall for a pet."

"You're not going to touch her." I seethed but cursed my reaction. My hand was fully blown now.

"Aw, you don't know where she is, do you? Which means she's still loose." The phone shifted as the moans from my father continued. "Here's what's gonna happen, *Constantine*."

Fuck. He knew my real name. How did he... My father.

"You're going to send me five hundred k for dear old daddy here, by the end of the week. Failure to do so will result in one removed limb for each day the money isn't in my account. Old and drunk as he is, I'm guessing he can only withstand a one-arm removal, but I'm willing to test it if you are?"

"Vincent, I swear to God—"

"In that time, I'll also be hunting for Amanda. Best take this time to clear up some of your assets if you want her back intact. You know how I love to keep their severed breasts as my trophies. One week, Connor. One week."

The phone hung up, and I stared at it. I had no move I could make. No plan to thwart him. For the first time since being locked inside my mother's cage, I was truly powerless.

CHAPTER SEVEN

KELLI

Holden hadn't said more than a few words after I mentioned that woman Shannon to him. Judging from his visceral reaction to her name, I assumed she was a bad breakup. It would make sense given the way he held me so tightly against his chest in his sleep. He must have thought I was her and didn't want to let her go. Perhaps *that* was what I was jealous of. Not of his love for another woman. I didn't know Holden from a hole in the wall. But I was jealous when I heard him say her name. Maybe I was envious of their love? I knew that a man would never dream of me like that. Perhaps, that was why her name stung so much.

It wasn't like I had a good track record when it came to being loved. My first sexual experience came from my high school English teacher. He used to write me sappy love sonnets but turned out to be a pervert who liked getting head from minors. High school boys were no different. Once they got their release, they moved on to their next conquest. Then, in adulthood, almost every family I nannied for over the last seven years had the father professing their undying love for me, only to give me the silent treatment as soon as I put out. Some would say I was a victim of predatory behavior, but I blamed myself. I was the idiot who kept falling for their lies. I was so desperate to be loved that I'd fall for even the weakest pickup line.

"Strawberry or cinnamon granola?" Holden startled me by showing up out of nowhere, holding two different brown, equally unappealing, packages.

"Oh, um, strawberry, I guess." He handed me the packet.

"Good. I hate strawberries."

I frowned. "Then why bother to offer me a choice?"

"After what you've been through, first dibs on this shit food is the least I can do."

His comment made me laugh. "How about first dibs on some more pain meds?" I flinched as I rubbed the makeshift splint. The dull throb was rearing its ugly head.

"Oh, right. Jesus. Sorry." He put his unopened granola beside me as he went downstairs to get the meds. I followed him, needing the chance to stretch my legs. It was cold in the sanctuary. A shiver seemed to always dance along my spine.

Holden went over to the floorboards that held the food and medicine stash and dug around until he found what he was looking for. I had to divert my eyes from clocking his ass as he did.

He handed me the pill, which I gratefully swallowed down dry. Just as he was about to put the floorboard back, however, he froze. His eyes were locked on the window to the right beside him. While it was boarded up, a crack between the boards let in the sun. He tiptoed over to the window and stared out. I stood still, not even daring to breathe.

After a moment, he turned his head over his shoulder. He raised a finger to his lips. He pointed at the door and then gestured for me to get down.

Suddenly the ache in my finger was gone, replaced by instant fear. I crouched behind the nearest pew and then flattened myself against the floor, trying my best to shimmy under the seat to hide. I listened as hard as I could for any clues as to what was going on. There was nothing besides the beating of my heart in my ears. My muscles all recoiled and tensed, ready to run, scream, kick, bite, whatever I had to do so I wouldn't be caged again.

Beside me, I heard Holden's soft footfalls as he inched his way to the door. While I couldn't see him from under the pew, I could imagine he had his gun out, ready to fire at anything that might burst through the doors.

A million thoughts were running through my mind, all at the same time. What if Connor or one of his thugs killed Holden? Should I try to run and find an escape out of the back of the church? There must be a rear exit; but would I have time to find it? Would they kill me on sight for trying to escape? Or would they put me back in the suitcase and deliver me to my butcher surgeon buyer? None of the options were good.

The crunch of dirt and debris under Holden's foot as he hovered by the door grounded me. It also provided some small comfort. It told me that he was just as tense and ready to pounce as I was. Then, a moment later, he moved to the other side of the church.

"Stay down," he whispered before he made his way upstairs. He either wanted to get a better look at what was outside or have the element of surprise if someone came in. Either way, I was a sitting duck.

Time seemed to move at a crawl as I stayed frozen, waiting for something to happen. Each second that went by felt like an endless loop of fear. The only sound from Holden was a short "fuck." Then, the creak of the stairs from him making his way back down. A moment later, he was in the pew beside me. He lowered himself to the ground so he could see me.

"What's going on?" I whispered.

"Someone is scouting the building."

"What do you mean?"

"I noticed a silver sedan earlier on my watch circle the block. Which, on its own, isn't any reason for alarm. But this is the fifth time I've seen it in the last four hours. That means someone is aware we are here, or at least suspects."

"What do we do? Do we make a run for it? I mean, we can't just stay here, right?"

Holden shook his head. "There isn't anywhere for us to go. Once we step outside the sanctuary, we'll have a target on our backs."

"Don't we already have that now? If there is a car circling the block, it means an attack is imminent. Doesn't it?"

"Maybe..."

"Maybe? How maybe?"

"It might not be Connor or his men scoping the place out, okay?"

I flinched at that news. "Who else would be looking for us? The Feds? You said they weren't coming for a few weeks."

Holden didn't answer right away. He seemed to be hedging on if he should share information. "It's complicated."

"Un-complicate it, Holden. Who the fuck is looking for us besides Connor?"

"It's not the Feds, that I know. But if it is who I think it is, it might be a good thing. Hopefully."

"You had better start talking, or I'm gonna get up and walk right out of this building and take my chances with whatever is out there."

To prove to him I wasn't joking, I started to shimmy my way from under the pew, making us almost nose to nose.

"You're not going anywhere." His voice was firm but not frightening. Quite the opposite. It felt oddly calming to hear the confidence in his tone. "I'll tell you everything. But first, let's make sure we don't get any visitors. Okay?"

"Fine," I pouted.

"I'm going to check the permitter again. Stay down."

HOLDEN

Kelli was scared, and I wasn't making her any less so. But until I knew for sure that the sedan wasn't going to make any sneak attacks, I wasn't going to take chances. If someone decided to step foot inside, I had to make sure it was the last step they took.

From my lookout on the second floor, I waited another solid hour. No signs of the sedan. That could only mean they got the intel they needed. Our clock had started. Company would be coming soon. I still wasn't sure if that was good or bad news yet. The only thing I did know was that I had to fill Kelli in.

Leaning over the balcony, I whispered to her. "Come up here, but duck low. Avoid the window at the back. It's not boarded up as well as the others."

She didn't need more instruction than that. A moment later, she was sliding out from under the pew. The shirt I'd given her to help keep her warm was dangling off her arms, hiding her hands from view. It was evident that she was scared as her eyes kept darting back to the door as though afraid someone would burst in at any moment. Valid. I had the same concern.

"Have you seen it again? The car?" she asked as she crawled toward me on her hands and knees, a task that must have been made harder on her with her injured finger.

"Nothing since that last sighting, which I think, might be a good sign. Or a bad one. Fuck. I don't know."

"Well, what do you know? Is it Connor? Did you see a driver?"

"It's not Connor. I doubt he'll come out of hiding any time soon. The driver I saw was about two hundred pounds too heavy to be Connor, but it might be one of his hired guns. Although how he would have traced us here, I don't know. We're a good hour away from where I rescued you. Unless they got us on a traffic camera or something. Shit. I didn't think about that." My mind was racing with possibilities.

"If it was Connor's man, wouldn't they have busted down the doors already?"

"They may be waiting for confirmation we're inside. Now, they may have it. I don't know how many times that sedan drove by before I clocked it. He might just be gathering evidence and the real attack will come when we aren't suspecting it."

"Then we have to leave? Right? We can't wait here for them to find us." Her eyes held her fear. But she had the most logical plan. If we'd been spotted, or even suspected to be in the sanctuary, the only sane thing to do would be to run. But there was just as much danger in leaving. If we hadn't been clocked, we would be once we stepped outside.

"Normally, I would agree with you," I said, "but... there might be another person looking for us."

"Who?"

I checked the window one last time before I sat in one of the chairs and gestured for her to do the same. She avoided the chairs and opted to sit on the floor. She hugged her knees to her chest, using the shirt to cover her bare legs. One glance at the chairs and then back at me. The bolted chairs. They spooked her. I'd forgotten.

"In theory, there might be someone else scouting the premises. There is only one person I gave this address to."

She gasped. "Who, Holden? Who the fuck knows we're here?"

I sighed. Telling her the truth would not go over well, but I had kept her in the dark long enough.

"I don't know for sure, but it may be that Malcolm Luxx guy. The one that saved Amanda. Since I'd already broken my cover, I took a shot in the dark and made a risky move, and left word at his residence. I know someone is still monitoring the place, even if he's not there, because his landscaping is always immaculate. Someone would get him the message..."

"How the hell would he help the situation we're in?" A valid question.

"My thinking was that if I could get Malcolm to testify about what he found in Connor's building, that he saw women caged, then it's an open-and-shut case."

Kelli scoffed. "Because no one trusts a woman's word. Need to make sure to get a man in there to legitimize the story. Is that it?"

"I never said it was fair. It's just how shit works." As much as I hated it, her assessment was spot on. Jury bias tended to believe a man's word over a woman's. Even a criminal's word. Twisted fucking world.

"So, you just called up a guy you don't know out of the blue and said meet me at an abandoned church?" The hysteria in her voice rose.

"No. Of course not." I flinched. "I sent a courier. And I never said it was a logical plan. I had a short window to make a move. Remember, my plan was never to save you. It was to take down Connor's ring. It was only while I was on the run with you when we were in the cab that I chose to reach out to Malcolm. Good or bad. But if it is Malcolm's guy scouting the property to make sure I'm legit, then there's hope that we might find a way out of this mess."

"How would this Malcolm guy change our situation? We would still be trapped here, wouldn't we?"

"Malcolm is rich. He has means. He could take us to a police station securely. And with his testimony, they'd have to believe you."

"What about *your* testimony?" Kelli asked. "You saw what they did? Wouldn't that be enough?"

"Maybe. But an attorney could also claim bias. That as an undercover cop, I planted information. That I baited Connor. I need a witness not tied to either of us. You don't get how weaselly these attorneys get. Criminals get off all the time on technicalities. I need this to be airtight."

"Why?"

I blinked at Kelli a few times, unsure if I'd heard her right.

"Why is this conviction so important to you?"

"Because he's a fucking monster. Do I really need more of a reason than that?"

Her eyes narrowed slightly. "No... it's just... this seems personal to you. That's all."

My jaw flexed. She was getting a little too close to the truth. Rising from the chair, I went back to my boarded window to peer through the cracks. Kelli crawled over to the other side of the church and looked out through the boards of another such window. "Silver sedan, right?"

She wanted to keep watch with me. My heart made a weird little flip-flop.

"That's right."

Kelli nodded once and then turned to focus her attention.

Whatever was about to happen, we'd be ready... In theory.

CHAPTER EIGHT

AMANDA

Was leaving the bathroom door wide open when I entered the shower cruel? Sure. Was it a "trauma" response to use my sexuality to try to forget every awful thing that had happened to me over the last few days? Probably. All I knew was that I didn't want to think about Kelli or the fear she must be experiencing. I didn't want to think about Connor planning out his revenge. I didn't want to imagine how long I'd have to stay hidden from the world. I didn't want to think at all. And the only way I knew how to escape pain and fear was to replace it with the ecstasy of an orgasm. If Malcolm didn't want to give me one because of whatever high moral horse he was on, I would give one to myself.

That was when I heard a soft moan. It was the sound that escaped your lips when you didn't mean it to. Glancing over my shoulder, I saw Malcolm sitting on the edge of the bed. Naked. Erect. Staring at me in the shower. His large hand was working his cock.

"You're not going to join me, are you?" I asked.

He shook his head, but his hand kept pumping.

"Fine. I'll join you." I turned off the taps and stepped out of the shower, water dripping over the floor. Malcolm's eyes grew wide as I approached him. I could see the internal struggle inside his mind. He wanted to respect me and leave before he did something stupid, but I wanted him to be stupid. I needed him to be stupid. With me.

"Amanda, we shouldn't," he tried. His voice was unconvincing while his eyes focused on my breasts as I came closer.

"*We* aren't doing anything. *I* am going to take advantage of you. Don't overthink it. Let's not deny ourselves something that we both want." I stood right in front of him, his hand still slowly working his cock as my fingers dug into the back of his hair.

"But—"

"No buts. Just suck." I leaned forward pressing my bare breast to his mouth. His lips parted instantly to take me in. After that, all his morals left his soul. He became unhinged and obsessed with every curve of my body. Sucking and licking, moaning and gasping as he explored.

He sat up taller to get better access to my tits, lifting me slightly as his fingers roamed over me. I let him explore. Closing my eyes, I relished in the pleasure of his tongue against my skin, the feel of his fingers as they dug into my hips.

From the corner of my eye, I caught our reflection in a mirror above the dresser. And in one quick flash, panic hit me. Suddenly, I was back in Connor's unit, bent over his bathroom sink as he took me. Everything tensed.

"What is it? Are you okay? This is too much, isn't it? I knew it." Malcolm tried to unlatch from me, but I held onto him.

"It's not you. It's the mirror." I pulled myself against his chest. "Connor, he used to..." I couldn't finish the sentence.

Malcolm pushed me back a little so he could look at me. Then, without warning, he went over to the dresser and pulled out a random shirt. So much for sexy time. I'd blown it. Again.

But instead of putting on the shirt, Malcolm wrapped it around his fist. Before I could ask him what he was doing, he drove his covered fist through the mirror. It shattered into pieces.

Carefully, he removed the shirt and discarded it onto the top of the dresser.

"There. No more mirror. It's just you and me. You're safe."

His words, coupled with such a gesture, hit me hard. For the first time in a very long time, I believed the words of a man. I felt safe. With him.

"Malcolm? Do you love me?"

His face distorted in confusion. "You know that I do."

Nodding, I walked over to the bed and lay on top of it. I rested on my elbows and spread my legs apart. "Then prove it. Get inside me. I need to feel how much you love me. Prove I can trust you. Don't fuck me. Love me."

I didn't have to ask him twice.

Within seconds, he joined me on the bed. His torso hovered over mine. I could see the question on his face.

"Yes, Malcolm, I'm sure. I want this. I want you."

He pressed his lips against mine gently before he shifted his weight and rolled over to the bedside table. There, he pulled out a drawer and withdrew a condom.

"Someone is prepared." I giggled.

"I was a Boy Scout." Malcolm tore off the top of the wrapper with his teeth and made quick work of rolling on the condom.

With eager hands, I reached for him, willing him to fill me.

He obliged and straddled my waist.

"Are you sure?" he asked. I knew if I showed any hesitation or had any doubt in my answer, he would respect my choice. But there was nothing to waiver on. I wanted him. All of him. To show him just how serious I was, I grabbed his cock and guided it to my entrance.

He hesitated for one moment, checking in with me yet again.

"Please," I whispered.

He pushed his hips forward and in one slow but deliberate motion, he was inside me. We both gasped at the sensation. My skin turned to gooseflesh as he moved gently in and out of me. My legs wrapped around his waist, locking him to me. I never wanted him to leave. I wanted this feeling to last forever.

His hands held mine against the bed as we kissed and moaned in pleasure.

"I have waited for so long to feel you like this," he said hot against my ear.

"And now that you have?" I locked eyes with him.

"You have ruined me for all time. You are literal heaven on Earth, and I never want this to end."

"It never has to. I'm yours, Malcolm. For as long as you want me." And I meant it.

"How about forever?" he countered.

"I could live with that."

He pushed deeper into me, and my eyes rolled back in my head. His mouth seized my right breast and sucked it so expertly that with his next thrust, I came hard and fast. I shook slightly as the sensation washed over me.

"My turn," he said devilishly. He slid his hands out of mine before he flipped me over onto my knees. My ass lifted to meet him. He wasted no time lining himself up to my seam. And eased in.

"Malcolm, you've shown me you love me. Now I want you to show me how you'd fuck me."

As though that was the permission he needed to have me the way he wanted, he gripped my hips and shoved into me so hard I let out a quick squeak of surprise.

"Do that again," I begged.

He complied not just once but several times in a row. Normally, I didn't care for it when a man jackhammered into me. But something about the angle was putting just enough pressure on my already swollen clit that I was already close to another release.

"Fuck! Yes, just like that," I shouted.

His hands moved to my breasts, cupping them as he pumped. The sound of his skin slapping against mine and the soft groans of his desire had me dampening.

"So... wet."

"You keep this up and I'm going to come again."

"Not without me you're not." He gripped my breasts hard, picked up his pace so he was rubbing against my G-spot in the exact right way, and a second later we were both shouting into the darkness.

He held me in his arms for a long time, still inside me. For a moment, I could have sworn I heard him cry. Yet, before I could ask, he rolled off me and collapsed on the bed.

"You have no idea how long I've been waiting to do that," he said with a sheepish grin.

"How long?" I asked, curling up beside him.

"Ever since the first day I saw you in high school."

"Wow. That is a long time." I ran my fingers over his pec. "Do you believe in fate? I mean, I never did before, but it's wild that we knew each other before all of this madness, isn't it?"

"Oh, I don't know. I've found that the world is small, despite how many people live in it. And maybe that *is* fate. Drawing the people together that are meant to be there."

I frowned. "By that logic, I was *meant* to be found by Connor?"

Malcolm shifted onto his side to look at me. "As much as I loathe that man, I can't deny that he was the person who brought me to you."

"Yeah, well, in our next lives, maybe you can be the one who is caged and tortured, and I'll be the one to save you."

He placed his warm hand over the side of my face. "He's never going to hurt you again, Amanda. You're safe now."

It was at that exact instant that a cell phone rang. The sureness in Malcolm's eyes vanished as they darted to the floor. The phone in his pocket went off again.

"Who could that be?" I asked.

"Only one person has that burner number. My scout."

"Answer it!" I shrieked.

The cell rang again before he made an audible grunt of annoyance as he left my side. Grabbing the cell phone from his pants on the ground, he punched the answer button.

"What have you found?"

This was it. Now, we'd find out if the lead he'd been sent was worth the paper it was written on—or if it had all been a setup.

MALCOLM

I listened intently as Rick, the private detective I'd hired, told me what he'd discovered at the sanctuary. I paced the floor, waiting for news. Amanda was quickly at my side, rubbing a hand against my back.

"Place is boarded up tight, just like the internet images showed. Took a bunch of shots. Those should be headed to the cloud soon. At first, I didn't see much. But I took a spin around the block at dusk. That's when I spotted two heads through one of the only windows not boarded up tight. One had dark hair, one blond."

My whole body tensed as the question tumbled out of my lips. "Could you tell if the two inside were men or women?"

"Couldn't make that out. Just the back of heads, in low light. Pics be headed your way soon. You might be able to tell better than me."

I ground my teeth together in frustration. "The remaining payment will be transferred once I see the shots." I hung up with him and ran my hands over my face.

"Well? Is Kelli there?"

"Not sure yet. Waiting for grainy pics to come in. All he knows is that there is a blond and someone with dark hair inside."

"The blond could be Kelli!" Amanda shrieked.

"It could also be Connor." At that, she took a step back.

"Oh. Right."

It was as though it only now clicked for her that this whole thing could be a trap.

"I want to see the pictures," she said after a moment.

"I do too." I took off the full condom and tossed it into the trash. Opening the dresser drawer, careful not to step on any glass, I pulled out two T-shirts. I tossed one at Amanda, who pulled it over her body. Then, I yanked on a pair of sweatpants and took her hand. Together we went to my computer to download the images.

"I mean, we don't know for sure the people in the sanctuary have anything to do with us," Amanda said as I turned on my computer. "It might just be homeless people."

"It's possible. But the odds of people being in the exact address that was sent to me?"

She gnawed on her bottom lip as the screen came to life.

Opening the cloud folder, I clicked the images. A permanent scowl was etched on my face. He wasn't lying. The images were poor quality, but there were two people inside that church. At the least.

"That's not Connor," Amanda said, staring at the back of one of their heads.

"You don't know that," I argued.

"I do. I know that monster's head. That isn't it. It's Kelli. Look." Amanda pointed to one of the rows of pictures. The face was still obscured, but there was one thing that wasn't. A bandaged finger.

"Jesus." I zoomed in on the image, and sure enough that was a finger wrapped in a bandage. The same finger we both saw get chopped off in real-time.

"That means this Holden guy did save her. And they need our help, Malcolm! We have to go to them. Now." She turned and started to head for the secret stairway, but I grabbed her by the wrist.

"Amanda, we can't go yet."

"Why not? We're wasting time. They need our help. Kelli needs medical attention."

"Yes, I understand that. But just because this doesn't appear to be Connor inside, it doesn't mean this isn't a trap. What if Connor sent this Holden guy there? What if this is a ruse to get us out of hiding? What if we're spotted by security cameras, and he finds out where we are? We aren't just going to march over to that church in broad daylight."

Her lower lip pouted at me. It was adorable.

"So, we go under the cover of night. Disguised, fully armed, and with an escape route mapped out if things go sour."

I raised an eyebrow at Amanda's foresight. "Exactly. Except for one small modification."

"Which is?"

"You're not going." I pushed out of the chair and went to the bedroom to get my gun. Amanda was right on my heels. As I assumed she would be.

"I *am* going, Malcolm. That note said specifically to bring me."

"Which is exactly why you'll stay here. Where it's safe. Just because we didn't see Connor in that photo, it doesn't mean he isn't there or puppeteering this entire thing. The only way I will enter that sanctuary is if your ass is planted on this bed until I return."

Amanda looked at me with an unreadable expression before she dropped to her knees, bowed her head, and whispered a bone-chilling, "Yes, Master."

Fuck. "Amanda, I didn't mean it like that."

"Didn't you, though? You talk a good game about wanting to respect me and how you're different from all the other men in my life, but you just proved that you aren't. At the end of the day, I'm still property to you. Something you can lock away from the rest of the world for only *you* to play with." She visibly shuddered. "How is that any different than what Connor wanted to do with me? At least Connor didn't bullshit me about his motives. I knew where I stood with him. I knew what he wanted. What I was being used for. But you? You gaslighted me into thinking you were this knight in shining armor. But really, you only do what you want. What I want doesn't matter. So, go, do your investigation alone. I'll be here, on my knees, waiting, like a good little girl for your return, ready to service your needs."

The tone of her voice was so broken and deflated that it nearly shattered my heart. The worst part was that I couldn't argue with her logic. She was right. I *was* behaving just like Connor.

CHAPTER NINE

HOLDEN

Hours passed with no sign of the sedan. That told me that whoever was in the car had what they needed. It was time to brace for company.

"Ok. Here's the plan," I whispered. "We're gonna move the supplies from the floorboards. Take them upstairs. In that emptied space, you're going to hide in there while I wait for whoever is going to walk through that door."

"You want to stash me in the floorboards?" Kelli's face paled.

"Just temporarily. It won't be as bad as you think. It's quite spacious under there. I mean, look at how much stuff was stashed."

"If it's so comfy, you do it. I have no desire to hide in a hole as small as a coffin."

I winced. Hearing it described like that didn't make it very appealing. "Look, it's the only place I can keep you safe. It's just until I clock whoever is coming. If it's Malcolm, you'll be out in no time, but if it's Connor... or one of his men, and I'm taken down, at least they can't get you. They won't know where you are as long as you stay hidden and quiet."

"So, you're just supposed to be the hero, and I'm supposed to cower in a corner? If it's so dangerous, shouldn't you be in there too?"

"There will barely be enough room for one person, let alone two."

Kelli crossed her arms, making sure her injured hand was on top. "Which is it, Holden? A minute ago, you said it would be sooo spacious. Now it's going to be too tight?"

"Spacious for you." I gestured to my wide torso. "I would never fit in there. I'm too big."

"That's what she said," Kelli joked. Despite all she'd been through, she still found a moment for laughter. I couldn't help but smile. She reminded me of Shannon. She could always make me laugh when times were hard. I shook my head to clear memories that tried to bubble to the surface.

"Let's just get it ready. If we don't have to use it, fine, but let's at least keep our options open while we still can."

Kelli seemed to notice the shift in my tone because she relented to my request. "Fine. But we're making it wide enough for you too."

I could tell there would be no point in arguing logic with her. She was determined to get us both to fit. Once she saw how narrow it was, she'd be forced to see it my way. But until then, I'd humor her.

Together, we went down to the main floor to work on the space. It took longer than I thought it would to move the items under the floorboards and carry them upstairs. We were forced to go slow and keep low to avoid the gaps in the boarded-up windows, but eventually, we managed to clean it out. When we were all finished, there was a space of about four feet by six feet and maybe three and a half feet deep—just enough room for *one* person. As predicted.

I laid down a bit of the carpet that I'd ripped off the floor from upstairs and put it down so she wouldn't have to lie in the dirt. It was dark, damp, and probably filled with spiders and mice, but it could work in a pinch as a temporary hideout.

"Give it a try. See if you fit. Then tell me how the hell you think I'm getting in there too."

Kelli stared at the hole in the ground and then back up at me. "The carpet is a nice touch. Makes it look more like a coffin now."

"It's not that bad."

"You get in it then," she huffed.

Sighing, I tossed my hands into the air. "Fine. I'll try to squeeze my body inside, but you'll see I'm too big to fit."

Reluctantly, I hopped down into the tiny space and was immediately overwhelmed with the percolating feeling of claustrophobia. I'd never been a huge fan of tight spaces, and this was tight. While I *technically* fit, my arms were pushed against both sides, and my head and feet were just about touching the edges. I'd need a shoehorn to get me out. At least it served to illustrate my point. We both wouldn't fit.

I was about to try to unstick myself from the spot when I noticed Kelli's face had gone white. Her whole body was rigid. Her eyes locked on the door.

"What is it?" I whispered.

"I just heard a car door shut," she whispered. "Fuck. And another one."

Someone was here. Our window to prepare had closed. "Get in here. Now." Before I could attempt to pry myself free to let her in, Kelli was climbing on top of me, pushing us both into the hole. There was no time to argue.

"Try and get the boards over," I said quietly, reaching as best I could to get around her and pull the wood over us.

Together, we managed to yank the boards over the hole, but it wasn't perfect. Panting, Kelli lay on top of me. Our chests pounded wildly against each other. Tiny pinholes of light came through, but outside of that, it was eerily dark in our hiding spot.

I tried, in vain, to reach for my gun. But I couldn't move my hand enough to release it from the holster without making too much noise. So, I did the only thing I could do. I wrapped my arms around Kelli and held her tight, willing the two of us to be as silent as death.

KELLI

Holden's arms wrapped around me was the only thing keeping me from screaming and trying to run out of the sanctuary, as there was no denying it—someone was outside.

My heart beat a mile a minute as did his. I could hear it thumping against my ear as I lay against his massive chest. His breath was hot against my neck while we both worked to control our breathing, terrified our inhalations would give us away.

At first, I didn't hear anything. I started to second guess if the noise I heard was even at the church, but that was when I flinched. A voice.

"You sure this was the place? Looks locked up tight." It was a man's voice I didn't recognize.

"You know of any other sanctuaries in the area?"

"No, but come on. This is a wild goose chase. Just because some Karen neighbor said she saw two people enter the building, we gotta drag our asses way out here? What a waste of our resources. Who the fuck cares if a couple of homeless people squat in an abandoned church?"

"Dispatch wants it checked out. I guess this 'Karen' is a politician's wife or some shit."

"Figures. I'll check the back. You check the windows."

The sound of retreating steps echoed over the space.

"They're cops," I whispered. "They can help, right?"

Holden shook his head. "Just stay silent for now."

We lay there together, locked in a weird embrace as we listened to the sounds of the doors rattling as they walked the perimeter.

"You see anything?" the deeper voice asked.

"Spiders and weeds. That's all that's around the back. Windows are all boarded up for the most part. The one that I could see through showed an empty church. There's no one here."

"Works for me. Let's get some grub. I'm starving."

We stayed motionless as the car started and they appeared to drive away.

"Fuck. That was tense," I said. I started to move the boards to get out of the hole, but Holden held me firmly.

"No. We're not moving until nightfall. This could be a trap. Some trick to lull us into coming out of hiding."

"Holden, I think you're overreacting. They're gone."

"Kelli, trust me. I've done this very maneuver. It's a tactic cops use. Lull the perp into a false sense of security. Then wait for them to reveal themselves. I don't trust it. We're not moving until the sun goes down, and that's final."

"But that's hours from now. What if I have to pee?"

He frowned. "We'll cross that bridge when we come to it. For now, we stay put." He tightened his grip, as though to make his point. I hated how nice it felt. Not just that someone was holding me, but that the person holding me cared enough to try to protect me.

"So, we're just supposed to stay here. For hours. That's the grand plan?"

"Yes."

I sighed. "Well, if this was any other circumstance, I'd say I would know of a few things we could do to pass the time, but..."

"I don't follow."

"Screwing, Holden. I was suggesting we could have sex until the sun went down." I could tell I'd just made him uncomfortable, as his grip around me loosened. "That shocks you, doesn't it?"

"Um, sort of. I mean, after everything you've been through, I would have thought sex would be the last thing on your mind."

I nodded against his chest. "That would be the logical reaction. But before Connor took me, I quite enjoyed sex. I was a bit of a serial dater, if I'm honest. Always trying to find someone I could have a real connection with, you know?"

"I'm not sure there is such a thing as a real connection with someone," Holden admitted. "If there is, I've never had it."

"Not even with Shannon?" His whole body tensed underneath

me. I could tell he wanted to escape the conversation, to walk away yet again at the mention of her name, but he was trapped under me. "She must have at least been a good lover to have that sort of impact on your emotions."

"It wasn't like that. Shannon was... *is* my sister."

"Oh. Sister. Right." A weird relief flooded through me. "I don't know why I jumped to a lover. A guy like you, I just figured you had a huge body count."

"Body count?"

"Yeah, like the number of people you've slept with. I usually have to lie about mine cause guys get all judgy if you say you've slept with more than three. But men? Men can fuck as many women as they want, and they are never considered a slut. Fucking double-standard."

"What *is* your actual body count?" Holden asked.

It was my turn to flinch. "Does Connor count?"

"No. Connor definitely doesn't count." His quick response made a butterfly float in my stomach.

"In that case, thirty-two." I paused waiting for the shock and horror to sink in. As it always did.

"Thirty-two? Wow. That's..."

"Slutty?" I countered. "How many women have you slept with, you hypocrite? Or men. I shouldn't assume your sexuality." *Please don't be gay.*

"I'm straight," he clarified.

My lips fought not to smile.

"As for 'bodies'... only two. Both in my early twenties. And I was drunk for one of them. Pathetic. I know. But I wasn't a very attractive teen. I was tall and scrawny, and my acne was a natural sex repellant. I joined the academy young. Only men there, well, and one lesbian. Then, I was sort of focused on my career, and then Shannon—"

"Shannon what? What happened?'

"She left us when she was seventeen. I don't like to talk about it, so can we change the subject?"

Damn. A runaway. That could screw a person up for sure. No wonder he didn't like to hear her name.

"Sure, we can go back to your sexual experiences. So, one drunken encounter. What about the other? How long ago was that?"

Holden let out a breath. "About seven years ago, I guess."

"Wow. So, you're like practically a virgin now."

He chuckled under me. "I guess."

"Hmm," I pondered. "With so few experiences, you probably don't have a favorite position or anything?"

His body shifted nervously under me.

"I'm not sure that matters for men. I understand it's harder for women, though."

I nodded. "Sure is. Of the thirty-two men who have been inside me, only two of them got me close to coming. Men aren't so good at finding the G-spot, let alone knowing how to manipulate it *if* they find it. You would think I wouldn't enjoy the act with those odds, but here is always the hope, you know? That one day I will find that person I can get off with. That a sexual relationship can be more than a one-sided experience. I mean, it happens all the time in romance books and movies. That has to be pulled from some real-world experience."

"I don't know. The cops I've seen portrayed on the screen don't reflect me so..."

"Valid," I laughed. I could tell Holden was feeling sorry for me, and I hated it, so I tried to shift the narrative. "It's not all bad, though. Foreplay, when it's done right, is super-hot for women. I get so wet and close to coming just in the ramp-up to sex a lot of the time. It usually falls flat in the act, so I have to get myself off in the bathroom afterwards."

"Foreplay. There's a novel idea. I should try that next time." Holden laughed.

"Yes. You should. The longer you can tease a woman, the slicker she'll get. Men are easy. You just touch their cock and they get hard. Women take more finesse."

"I don't know about that. I don't think just a touch—"

To prove my point, I snaked my hand down and cupped his crotch. Within seconds, his erection was evident.

"As I was saying, men are easy," I said, pulling my hand back, smiling ear to ear.

"Fuck. That's embarrassing."

I shrugged. "It's just how men are. Always down to fuck."

"Still. Hate to prove your theory about men."

"It's proven well before you." I saw his eyes close as though he were trying to will the blood out of his cock. My lips twitched as a devilish thought crossed my mind. "I assume that's going to be rather painful now. Being so hard and pressed against me like this, with nothing you can do about it?"

"Little bit." He chuckled.

"So, if I were to do this, would that help at all?" I moved my waist up and down over him.

"Fuck. No. Definitely not helping me calm down."

"Who said I was trying to do that?" I raised one eyebrow. "Let me finish what I started."

"I'm sorry?" God, he was adorably naïve.

"I'm going to get you off, Holden." My good hand went back down to his crotch. He moaned against my touch. His hips rose to find my hand, as though drawn to it by a magical force he couldn't control.

Holden gritted his teeth together as though trying to resist the feeling. "You don't have to, Kelli. I just need a minute to calm down."

"I know I don't *have* to Holden. I want to. Now shut up and let me give you a hand job."

"Kelli, I don't want to take advantage of the situation. You've been through too much. I'll be okay. Really. I just need a second."

I rolled my eyes. "You don't get it, do you, Holden? I want to do this. I know it makes no sense, but can you please let me have a moment to do something I want to do, instead of something I'm being forced to do? Let me take some of my power back as a woman."

He couldn't argue that. He nodded his consent, so I undid his zipper.

CHAPTER TEN

CONNOR

Have info you may want.

I glanced at my burner. It was Carlos's number. That fucker. Did he not realize I knew about his betrayal?

Vincent ratted you out. Count your days, Carlos.
I'm coming for you.

The dots bounced a few times, then retreated as Carlos wrote and rewrote his reply.

So, you don't want to know where K and A are?
Interesting.

My hand balled into a fist, but curiosity got the better of me.

I'm listening.

I had eyes on M's house. A courier arrived. Before he could deliver the package, I convinced him, by means of two broken fingers, to divulge the contents. An address. With instructions to bring A. Two local beat cops just scouted the address. One of them ours. He confirmed he saw evidence of someone inside. How much is that address worth to you? I know V would pay a pretty penny for one of your pets. One chance. What's your offer?

That fucker. He was playing both sides. Thanks to Vincent's call, I knew he was bought out for a mere hundred K, but I also knew I had one reply to make this deal.

500K

The dots bounced again as I held my breath.

Stay tuned. We'll see what V comes back with. Highest bidder wins.

Fuck. I should have bid higher.

CHAPTER ELEVEN

AMANDA

I sat on my knees. The insult I'd hurled at Malcolm about my being his property hurt him more than I would have expected. The way he was looking at me... so disgusted. Not with me, but with himself. His reaction confused me. I'd said something hurtful. Why hadn't he already smacked me across the face? Why were his hands not balled into fists? Why wasn't he turning red with rage? Why wasn't he shouting at me?

Instead, Malcolm sank to his knees to look me in the eyes.

"Amanda, is that really what you think of me? That I want to cage you, like Connor?"

I lifted my hands and gestured vaguely around. "Is this not a cage? It may have cushy amenities like bedsheets and access to food, but at the end of the day, is it any different than his cage if I'm never allowed to leave?"

"It's for your protection."

"Kelli is the one who needs protection right now. She's being held in some abandoned church by God knows who, and she needs our help. And you want me to sit here like a good little girl while you go and try to be a knight in shining armor. Well, I don't want to do that. I want to help. I want to have some control over my fucking life!"

The tears came out of nowhere as all my pent-up fear and anger bubbled to the surface. The last few days of non-stop adrenaline were catching up to me. Guttural sobs escaped my lips. I was a bomb of emotions going off, and Malcolm was the sole person taking the hit for everyone who had ever hurt me.

His strong arms pulled me to his chest. At first, I flinched, unprepared for such a reaction. But then, I collapsed into him. I let him hold me until all of the tears had run dry.

"I'm just so tired, Malcolm." I sniffed. "Tired of being scared. Of waiting for the bottom to drop out. I'm tired of hiding in the moments of pleasure with horrible men, pretending that this time, this time things will work out." I wiped away a tear. "All my life, it's been a struggle to keep the idea that a better life is just on the horizon when the world keeps dragging you back underwater. And I'm tired of kicking against the current. I want to walk on land. I want to stop struggling. And I know Kelli feels the same, Malcolm. I got out, thanks to you. I want to return that favor to her. I want to save her. I don't want her to lose hope. Not like I did."

Malcolm stared at me, cocking an eyebrow upward and silently asking for clarity.

"When Connor stuck me in that dog kennel, that cold metal box... and then the fire alarms went off...." I struggled to get the words out. "He told me flat-out that he wasn't going to have time to save me. I was going to burn inside that box. Naked and alone. I lost it. All will to live. I was ready to die. I accepted my fate. I completely shut down." I shook my head, trying to clear the memory of smoke filling my lungs. My stomach lurched as I remembered the sense of dread. "And then, out of nowhere, you were there. This wave of hope washed over me, replacing the fear." I let out a small laugh. "Honestly, I didn't believe you were real at first. I thought my mind had made you up as yet another coping strategy. Even now it's hard to believe I didn't die in that building."

I shifted so I could look him in the eyes. "Even though I'm out of Connor's cage, I'm still not free. I'm still drowning, and I can't find the shore."

"And saving Kelli will get you to land?" He was trying hard to follow my rambling.

"If I can help get Kelli to safety... If I can make her struggle come to an end, it is worth whatever cost that might bring. *Whatever the cost.* She was beaten, raped, and lost a finger because of me, Malcolm. You don't get how much that guilt weighs on me. I don't care if it's a trap. I don't care if I'm killed. I just want to make one thing I do in my life matter."

Malcolm took my hand in his and brought it slowly to his lips. "Okay."

I blinked at him several times. "Okay? You'll let me go with you to the sanctuary?"

"On one condition."

A sigh escaped me. "Which is?"

"You learn how to fire a gun first."

There it was again. That pesky feeling that I thought was long dead. Hope.

A huge grin slid across my lips. "Deal."

MALCOLM

Was it insane to bring Amanda along with me and follow the instructions of Kelli's new captor? Absolutely. But Amanda had argued her point. She had lost her autonomy with Connor. I was going to give it back to her. But this time, I would make sure she had the skills to take his ass down, if it came to it.

While I didn't exactly have a shooting range under my house, and I was not going to risk taking her outside to shoot, I did have something at least vaguely comparable.

"A video game?" Amanda asked when I brought her into the living room and opened the cabinet to reveal several gaming consoles.

"You got a better idea?" I gestured around the enclosure.

"No. I suppose not. So, how do we do this?" She picked up a bulky-looking controller and started pushing the buttons.

"Well, not with this, for starters. You can't learn to shoot with a controller like that. Believe it or not, there aren't toggle switches on a real gun."

"You don't say?" She smirked. "Okay, what am I using then, smartass?"

Instead of answering her, I opened a second cabinet door with a much older and smaller TV. "Games with gun-style controllers are hard to find these days. Most of the functionality of the lights they used for aiming at targets stopped working when flat screens and LCDs came out. It has to do with the reflective surface versus a tube style. Basically, as TVs got better these types of controls got worse." I held up the corded gun control and handed it to her.

"Wow, that's surprisingly heavier than I would have thought."

I nodded. "I added weights to the bottom. It will affect your aim if you're not used to the right weight."

"I'll take your word on that." She aimed at the blank screen and pulled the trigger. "So, what are we playing? *Duck Hunt*?"

"A little game called *Time Crisis*."

"Fitting. Seeing as that's exactly what we're under. A time crisis."

For the next several hours, I tried—with some success—to teach Amanda how to aim and shoot at NPCs. At first, she missed more than she landed and was quite frustrated at herself... until I said one thing as she was aiming.

"Pretend it's Connor."

Her aim improved almost instantly. When she grew confident, we moved on to her holding one of my guns, unloaded and with the safety on.

"Feel the difference?" I asked her as she lifted the gun to point at the television that was now off.

"Yeah. Definitely different."

"Pulling the trigger on that will feel different as well. Keep your eyes open and aim for the largest body part you can. Lots of important organs and stuff around here," I said, pointing to my abdomen. "That's a good first place to hit if you don't think you can get a headshot. If you can't kill him, at least you can hurt him. Then, when he's down, take secondary aim. Wound, then kill. Got it?"

She nodded as she held the gun out. She looked fierce as fuck.

"Okay. Load this bad boy up, and let's go," she said, handing me back the gun.

Shaking my head, I took it from her. "Not yet. Two a.m. That's when the world and nightlife are asleep."

Amanda huffed. "That's hours away from now."

"I know. I'm sorry. But if it means we can rescue Kelli from under her captor's nose?"

"Fine." She pouted. "But what are we supposed to do until then?"

I glanced back at the TV. "We could do some more gun training."

Her eyes narrowed. "There's actually another weapon I'd like to explore. If you're up for it?"

"Oh? What did you have in mind? Knives? I'll be honest, I'm not very good with a knife. I mean, I can whittle a stick, but that's about as far as my skills go."

"No, I was thinking of another potentially deadly weapon. One that gets hard like wood." She sauntered over to me, took the gun from my hand, and placed it on the ottoman. "I wouldn't mind a repeat of what we did earlier."

Before I could answer, her hand surrounded my cock, which sprang to life at her touch. The guttural noise that escaped my lips should have embarrassed me, but it didn't. She had that power over me. To switch my emotions at the touch of her fingers.

"Your wish is my command. Where do you want me?"

"Let's start in between my legs and go from there."

That, I could do.

CHAPTER TWELVE

HOLDEN

Of all the places I'd dreamed of getting a hand job, under the floorboards of an abandoned sanctuary wasn't one of them. And yet, here I was, lying on the ground on top of some gross, torn carpeting, with Kelli, a woman I had just met, on top of my chest, stroking the length of my cock in such a way that I was going to blow my load at any second. It was torture: both needing to get off but never wanting the feel of her hand against me to stop.

"You're so hard," Kelli whispered. "If I had enough room, I'd totally blow you, because damn, I bet you taste divine."

"Ung" was the only guttural noise I could make. I was lost to the feeling of her pumping. My hips rose and fell with her, searching for the release that was imminent.

"May I kiss you?" she asked, taking me aback. "You have soft-looking lips. I'm curious what they taste like."

Again, no words could escape my lips. Instead, I nodded vigorously. The second her lips touched mine, I exploded in her hand. I moaned far too loudly for someone trying to hide as my release spread out of me and ran down her fingers.

"Fuck." I panted against her lips as she continued to kiss me. Her tongue shot inside my mouth, and I swear I saw stars. "That was... fuck, that was amazing."

“My turn.” She giggled. Shifting on top of me, she lowered her hand to her waist.

“Oh, let me,” I tried.

“No. No one goes inside but me right now. I have a wee bit of trauma to heal from. Please don’t take offense. I just can’t...”

“No. No, of course. That makes total sense. Is there anything I can do to, er, help?”

She seemed to consider my question seriously.

“Not sure if you can reach, given our close quarters, but if you wanted to try and find a tit to fondle,” she suggested.

“On it.” My hunger to touch her grew tenfold. I would find a way to her breasts, even if I tore a muscle to do it.

While it took far more finagling than I would like to admit, we found a way to meet both of our needs. Her, working her clit with her fingers still covered in my semen, while I cupped her breast, trying to time my touch with her moans.

“Holden...” Her breath was so soft. So desperate. She was close. My hips lifted off the ground, pressing her own hand deeper into herself, and a moment later, she gasped and shook slightly against her fingers. She had never looked more beautiful.

“Well, that was a first,” she said once she’d recovered.

“Getting off under a church?” I laughed. “Me too.”

“That too, I suppose. I just meant...” She grew quiet. Her head seemed to try to bury itself against my chest.

“Just what?”

She took a deep breath and said, “Just getting off with the guy’s help. Usually, it’s a solo effort, if you know what I mean. But just now, with you touching me, and that move at the end... well, that was fucking epic. Thank you. It’s nice to know I’m not broken.”

Her tone was in jest, but I could tell she sincerely believed that something was wrong with her.

“Well, if we’re sharing firsts,” I admitted. “That’s the first time I’ve cum from a kiss. Fuck. That was intense. Talk about soft lips. Yours are like goddamn pillows, and I just want to linger there forever.”

"Really? Huh. Most guys don't pay much attention to my lips. They want my tits or my ass."

"Those are equally lovely, but if I had to pick one feature about you that has made my dick twitch inappropriately, it would be those damn lips. They are perfection."

"Perfection? That's not something I hear about myself, like ever." She chuckled. "Funny, isn't it? All the stuff people hate about themselves, and we never consider what we look like might appeal to someone else."

"Self-loathing is a coping skill. A defense mechanism. The one reliable thing in an unpredictable world. Hatred will always be there, even when hope isn't."

"Well, shit. That's depressing. Honest, but depressing."

"That's life in a nutshell, I'm afraid."

"Ain't that the truth," Kelli agreed. "So, now what do we do?"

"Once we hit nightfall, we can get food and use the bathroom before we come back here. Just until we know for sure we don't have more company."

I felt her nodding her head against my chest. "So, we stay here and basically cuddle for a few hours? That works for me."

My arms wrapped around her waist and held her against me. "Me too."

Be very careful, Holden. You might catch feelings without meaning to. This was a one-time thing to release some stress. Don't get used to the feeling of her on top of you. This is not your endgame.

I clenched my teeth together to try to remember my mission. Hard to do under the soft sounds of her breathing against my neck. I was so fucked.

KELLI

As I lay against Holden's chest, acutely aware of how protective his arms felt around me, I struggled to reconcile my emotions. What

I'd admitted to Holden moments ago about never getting off with a partner in the room was true. My releases always came after the guy had fallen asleep or were expertly faked so as not to inadvertently trigger male ego anger. I knew my ability to get off was my issue and not theirs. But I could never seem to get out of my own head long enough to get there.

So, having a release with Holden was unexpected. To have it with a stranger in this fucking hole in the ground after escaping a sex trafficking ring was a whole different level of messed up. What did that say about me as a woman that I could think about getting off when I should have been scared shitless?

Maybe that was part of it, though. Holden didn't scare me. He should. Logically, I knew that. I didn't know him at all. Add to the fact that he was working for a sex trafficking ring, undercover or not. Then, on top of that, he was three times my size... exactly the sort of man women should cower from, and yet, there was a softness in the way his eyes met mine. Tenderness when he held me. I knew that I was mistaking general human kindness for attraction, but the way my stomach fluttered when I looked at him, I was starting to question my sanity.

"Holden, tell me something real. Something not connected with Connor or this fucking world I've found myself stuck in. Tell me something normal from your past."

"Um, I'm not sure I had a normal past. My life story isn't the stuff of bedtime stories."

"Whose is? That's what makes it real. Come on. Humor me. What else are we gonna do to kill the time?"

Holden shifted under me, as though he were uncomfortable.

"You don't have to talk about your sister," I added.

"I wasn't planning on it. No offense, but she's sort of off-limits."

"Understood. I have people like that in my life too."

"Like who?" he asked.

I frowned. "You're trying to change the subject."

He sighed. "Clearly, it didn't work. All right. Fine. Um, let's see.

I grew up in a trailer park. We were dirt poor. Some months we had running water, and some we didn't. Food being available was hit or miss, depending on how much my dad drank through his paycheck. Is that the sort of thing you want to hear?"

I shrugged against him. "Whatever you'd like to tell me about. I'm curious about how you became who you are."

"You mean, how did such a great guy end up working for horrible men?"

"I didn't say that."

"You didn't have to. It's a logical question. My past comes down to being cold, hungry, and poor. Always on the back foot. Then, in my teens, I figured out that I was pretty good at stealing things. Made some quick cash from a few big sales. I'm not proud of it, but hunger motivates you like nothing else does. After a big cash out one day, I realized I had to make a choice. Keep going down the same path of crime or try and straighten myself out. I was still living in that shit trailer park. I knew I couldn't stay there anymore, especially after my sister..." He cleared his throat, as though he remembered he wasn't supposed to mention her.

"So, with my wad of cash, I applied to the local police academy. It was a twenty-week program. Out of town. Housing and meals included. It was a no-brainer. The clear road out of the hell I was living in. And maybe pay back my debt to society for all the thieving I'd done."

"What did you steal?" I asked, completely invested.

"Jewelry at first but finding the real stuff was harder to do in my neighborhood. So, I'd walk into the city. Maybe snatch a few necklaces off women on the train while they were on their phones or something. I moved on to simple burglaries, taking TVs and game consoles, but the money wasn't worth the risk. That shit is so cheap now. That's when I started lifting artwork and vases. Some of it was worth thousands."

"Wow. Really? I wouldn't know good art from bad if it hit me in the face."

I felt his chin nod against the top of my head. "Art is

subjective. But it's one of the only things I was good at as a kid. I was in the special art program at my high school. It was me and six girls. They were drawing flowers and self-portraits. And here I was, this trailer-trash kid painting in a Rococo style. Where the hell that came from, I have no clue."

"Roco?"

"Rococo," he clarified. "It's a French style of painting. I mean, it wasn't *exactly* like that, because how could I paint in a style I'd never seen before? But that's what my teacher compared it to. I painted old, rich architecture shit. Fine detailed painting. So detailed that from a few feet away, it would look like you were looking at a photo, not brush strokes." He sighed, the movement causing his chest to rise with me atop it. "I don't know, maybe I was trying to manifest a better place to live. A stable framework or some shit. I just know that when I was painting, I wasn't poor. I wasn't hungry. I was transported somewhere else. It was a bright light in a dark world."

"That's amazing." My eyes widened at learning this side of him. "I'm not talented at anything."

Holden chuckled. "I wouldn't say that. Your hand job game is something to write home about."

I felt myself laughing. A real laugh. It was healing.

"Did you have any hobbies or passions before..." he asked.

"Before Connor destroyed my life?"

"Yeah." Holden held me tighter for a moment. I tried to ignore the warmth it sent through my limbs.

"When I was little, I wanted to be a vet. But I think that was more because animals were kinder than humans in my life. It was a pipe dream, though. I don't have book smarts for vet school. I'm not wired that way. So, I did what every cliched woman with no book smarts does. I latched onto men who could give me a place to live and worked just about every odd job there was to pay the bills." I cringed at the memories of some truly shitty jobs. "But that's when I found nanny gigs. It provided me with the two things I needed: a job and a place to live. Who cares if I had to constantly deal with the dads hitting on me? That was easy when you had a bed to sleep in, ya know? The irony in all of this is that the ad Connor lured me into his cage with? I really thought that place was going to be my fresh start. What an idiot."

"Once this is over, you'll get the restart you're looking for, Kelli. I promise."

"Mhmm." I sighed. I wouldn't get that. He and I both knew it. Right now was merely a respite before all hell broke loose again; but for the moment, all I could think about was how nice his arms felt as they held me close, and before I knew it, I was sound asleep.

CHAPTER THIRTEEN

CONNOR

The picture of a severed toe Vincent sent me could have been anyone's. Hell. It could have been an image he found on Google. But I knew it wasn't. Vincent wasn't the sort to miss an opportunity to torture someone. Fuck, I got some of my own pet control ideas from him. That's how I knew that the toe staring back at me on my phone belonged to my father. And I knew he didn't have a surgeon on call to reattach it like I did.

The image was meant as a reminder of the timeline. One week to get him five hundred K. But if I were also paying Carlos for information on Amanda's whereabouts, I would not have the assets available to pay them both in such a short turnaround. While I was wealthy, those assets were protected and buried in layers upon layers. Unraveling that took time, not to mention coming out of hiding to authorize such large sums. Which meant, I had some things to consider.

Rubbing my temples, I pondered my options. I could bite the bullet and pay them both, which would risk my getting caught by the Feds with the money trail. I could call their bluff and let the cards fall where they may. It wasn't like my father and I had the world's best relationship. Was saving his drunk ass even worth the risk? The second I gave in to any of Vincent's demands; I would be forever under his thumb.

As for Carlos... the lead on Amanda could be fake. A ruse to get money out of me. Even if the address was legit, should I risk that large an investment on a single pet? Should I let her go as well? Be done with the distraction? I should, yes, but could I? I pulled at the strands of my hair. Would it be better to focus on my pets in Canada and start my empire from the ground up again? Give Vincent exactly what he wanted by fleeing the country.

Or maybe, I'd just kill Vincent and Carlos.

I liked the sound of that one the best. The only issue was how. I didn't know where either of them were. *Fuck.*

Grabbing my phone, I made the easiest of the decisions in front of me and replied to Vincent's picture.

Happy chopping. You will get nothing from me. Count your days.

In one text, I'd sentenced my father to a brutal death. Vincent would keep his word and rip him apart limb by limb, and yet, the choice was surprisingly easy. Cathartic even. Finally, that man would be out of my life. I wouldn't have to burden myself with paying off his debts or live with his drunken pleas for past transgressions. Nor would I be the one to end it. It was all my father's fault if I thought about it. His inaction to my mother's cruelty when I was a boy turned me into this... thing. It was only fitting that my inaction now would be the end of who he was. After all this time, he was finally getting his comeuppance. Vincent was doing me a service.

One of the financial burdens was now off my shoulders. What about the other? It was time to decide on Amanda's fate. If Carlos had an address to where she was hiding, would I want to find her? After all, she had single-handily placed me in this fucking position. Hiding like a rat. And yet, even after all of that, the image of holding her in my arms, of pressing her full lips to mine... my cock twitched at the thought. *Fuck.* I would pay Carlos and take back what was mine, damn it.

I paced the room.

No. I shook my head. I had to get her out of my mind. Before she ruined every operation that I owned. I had to be smart. I had to lay low. Maybe for a few years before I could take Vincent out when his guard was down. But I'd have the last word. Carlos would get what was coming to him eventually, and one day even Malcolm. They would all pay for what they'd done to me. Until then, I needed to be patient. And if life in a cage had taught me anything, it was patience.

CHAPTER FOURTEEN

AMANDA

Sex with Malcolm was never going to get old. The first time wasn't a fluke. He knew how to touch me in all the right ways. And I clearly knew how to send him over the edge. As I sucked off the last bits of his release from his cock, I knew I was reciprocating his needs. There was an immense sense of power and pride in that knowledge.

"Amanda, that was..." Malcolm said once my lips came off him.

"Yeah. It sure was. We need to do that again."

"Absolutely. I just need a minute."

I sat up on my elbows and glanced at the clock. "No. I didn't mean today. We need to leave soon. Once Kelli is safe, we can fuck like bunnies."

Reality hit us both.

Malcolm let loose a reluctant sigh and pulled me to him, as though he never wanted to leave this ottoman. Truth be told, I didn't want to either.

Needing to refocus, I pushed off him. "Let me take a quick shower while you get the guns ready?"

He gave me a nod. I rose from the ottoman to head to the shower, but his hand grabbed my waist. He pulled my stomach to his lips and held me gently there for a moment.

"We *will* find Kelli. I promise."

Running my fingers through his hair, I pressed a tender kiss to his head. "I'm choosing to believe you. A first... Me... Trusting a man's word. Miracles do happen." His hands tightened around my waist again as he gave me one last embrace.

I don't know if Malcolm truly understood how important it was to me to save Kelli. If we could rescue her, then somehow, this whole ordeal would have been for something. I wasn't naive enough to believe that her being saved would magically heal all the trauma that came with being caged, but it felt like a first step. An imperative first step. If we got to the sanctuary and she was dead... a part of me would die too. There had to be a reason I went through this hell. There just had to be.

MALCOLM

To say making love to Amanda was the best thing I'd ever experienced was an understatement. I still wanted to have her in countless ways, but she was right. Now was not the time. The only way either one of us could move forward with our lives was to finish this rollercoaster ride. And if today brought the end of us, at least I would die with the knowledge of Amanda's love.

Our plan to head to the sanctuary hadn't changed since we'd first discussed it. We'd go during the witching hour, using the back entrance, and pray no one would hack my surveillance footage here at the house. Taking the DBX out of the garage was a huge gamble, but I didn't trust using a car service. I didn't want anyone to know where we were headed. Besides, if Kelli was inside, we'd need a fast way to get us all the hell out of there. My Florida safehouse stood at the ready, if we were successful.

The missing piece to this jigsaw was this "H" person. Could they be trusted? We were walking into the situation blind, whether

"H" was a friend or foe. But we wouldn't be going unarmed. It was the only saving grace.

"I'm ready. Are you?" Amanda asked as she came out of the bedroom. Her hair was dripping onto one of my shirts. The sweatpants I'd given her were rolled several times at the waist so the legs wouldn't drag. Even though the clothing was swimming on her, she looked radiant.

"Yeah. I'm ready." I pointed to a pair of hiking boots. "Try those on. They were Darcy's, probably the only thing here that will fit you."

"Wow. Clothing *and* shoes. What a treat." She slipped on the boots. "A little loose, but they'll work. Okay. What now?"

I grabbed the bag of gear and weapons and then reached for her hand. "Now, we drive. In theory, we'll be there within the hour. But, Amanda, if we get there… if things smell fishy…"

"I know. Plan's off." Her hand squeezed mine. "Thank you for trying. It's not something I'm used to."

"Hey, it's you and me now. We're in this together. No matter what happens. You can trust me."

She shot me a small smile. "I'm still grappling with that one. But let's get through today, shall we?"

"Yes. Let's."

Next stop, rescue Kelli, or die trying.

Driving out of the safehouse was uneventful. Despite being on edge, and looking over our shoulders a million times, it didn't appear we had been followed. Two blocks from the address given, I pulled over and stopped the car.

"What is it? Do you see something?" Amanda whispered. She was in the back, sitting on the floor yet again. Her idea.

"No. The building is a few blocks north of us. Now that we're here, I'm not sure if the smarter play is to go on foot from this point or to drive up to the place in case we need a fast getaway."

Amanda seemed to be debating the same thought as she popped her head up and stared out the windows. It was dark outside with only a few scattered streetlights working. The place I'd parked was deliberately in the shadows.

"I could run two blocks if I had to. Could you?" she asked.

"I could."

"So, we go on foot. Try to get a leg up."

I gave her a nod. That was my gut feeling as well. It was nice to have it confirmed. "Okay. Your safety is on, yes?"

Amanda reached down to pull out the gun tucked into the back of her sweats. "Yes. We're good."

"Okay. We're going to get out of the car as silently as we can. Don't slam your door. Stick to the shadows and follow close behind me. If anything goes sour, anything at all, get your ass back to this SUV with or without me. The spare key is under the mat. You get the hell out of here and don't look back. Understood?"

Amanda scoffed in the darkness. "You think I'm leaving you behind?"

"If shit hits the fan? Yes. This is a non-negotiable item. I'll take us back to the safehouse right now if you aren't on board with that. I agreed to *try* to save Kelli, but I won't risk losing you to do it. The only way I'll attempt it is if I know you'll make sure to run if things go south."

She let loose a huge huff. "Fine. But it's not going to come to that. We're all getting out of this one alive. Except for Connor. If he's there, one of us kills him. Preferably me."

An overwhelming sense of pride bubbled in my chest. "Yes, Amanda. That is understood. Connor is yours to kill."

She gave me a devilish grin.

"Okay," I said, unlocking the doors. "Let's go save Kelli."

CHAPTER FIFTEEN

HOLDEN

I shouldn't have been holding Kelli so tightly. I knew there wasn't any room to do much else with my arms, but I should have at least been respectful and put them by my side. Yet, no matter how many times I tried to move them, they refused to budge. They'd locked themselves around her as she slept softly against my chest.

While my dating life wasn't as prolific as hers, I had held a woman in my arms before. Still, Kelli felt different somehow. Right. My hands lay perfectly on the small of her back, as though they were made to fit there. *Don't read into it, Holden. You're protecting a civilian from a dangerous situation. We protect and serve. That's all this is. I'm just doing my civic duty.*

Accepting a hand job, however, was not part of my role. That was a moment of weakness. One I couldn't allow to happen again. She had been fucked over too many times in her life. I wasn't about to add to that. I had to remember that I was here to protect her.

And for the moment, I was succeeding at my job. She was safe. Hidden. How long we could survive in these conditions remained to be seen, but there was comfort in having a hiding space. Something would have to give soon, though. Either Malcolm would show up... or Connor and his men would. The odds that both would stay off the radar weren't realistic. On the flip side, if neither came, we'd run out of food within the next week and a half. Then what?

At some point, I must have drifted off to sleep, as well, because the next thing I knew, I was being shaken awake by Kelli.

"Wake up!" she whispered. "Someone's here."

At that, my eyes darted open. My arms became a vice around her waist. *No. They won't take her from me.*

With great care, I listened for a sound, but I didn't hear anything.

"I heard glass shatter." Kelli's voice was barely above a whisper and still, it felt like she was shouting.

I nodded, trying to signal her to stay quiet.

The minutes ticked on as we lay there, frozen in fear. Every breath we took I worried would give us away. On and on we waited for something. Anything to confirm that the danger our bodies were reacting to was real. But nothing came. "Maybe it was a kid messing around?" I whispered.

That's when we heard a new sound. A voice. Low. Too quiet to make out.

The sound was coming from the back of the church. The broken glass made sense now. They must have broken it in the door to access the lock. The desk haphazardly shoved in front of that door would be no match for someone determined to get inside. Which these intruders seemed to be intent on.

The loud scrape of the desk moving against the floor confirmed they were inside.

"Can you reach my gun?" I whispered as quietly as I could. From this angle, I'd have to move too much, and I didn't want to risk a sound. Kelli nodded as she shifted her hand toward my holster.

Once it was in my hand, I felt slightly better. Slightly.

The intruders weren't quiet as they moved into the sanctuary. Their hand had been blown by the sound of their entrance. It wouldn't take them long to determine there wasn't anyone inside.

But they would likely find the food and provisions we'd stashed on the balcony and could put two and two together that we were here at least for some stretch. I could only hope they weren't planning to wait and see if we came back. We'd starve in this hole.

"Someone was here," a deep male voice said. "MRE packaging. Whoever it was, had enough forethought to plan ahead."

"Could they still be here? Just hiding?"

A female voice. Odd. On top of me, Kelli's head lifted off my chest. Her curiosity was peeked as well.

"Let's check the balcony," the man's voice suggested.

As we listened to the sound of their feet going upstairs, Kelli pressed her lips against my ear and whispered one word. "Amanda?"

For the first time since we'd landed here, I felt a wave of hope. If that was Amanda, then the deep voice with her had to be Malcolm. Yet, we needed confirmation before we made our hiding spot known.

"Wait," I whispered back. She nodded, seeming to understand the need to make sure. As though the universe knew what we were waiting on, the woman spoke again.

"Kelli? Are you here? It's Amanda. We're here to rescue you."

Before I could stop her, Kelli sat up and lifted the floorboards off, betraying our hiding spot.

"Amanda! We're here!" Kelli scrambled free of the hole as I worked to do the same.

"Malcolm! Look. She's here. She's safe! We found her!"

Climbing out of the hole, I watched as Kelli ran to meet Amanda as she came down the stairs. The two of them embraced and wept while Malcolm and I sized each other up. He was a big guy, like me. His weapon was out and ready, as was mine.

"You must be H?" he asked.

"Holden." Neither one of us made a move to shake hands as we watched each other's moves.

"Nice to meet you," Malcolm said.

I let out a short grunt. "We've met before."

Malcolm cocked his head. "We have?"

"You stole my art as a teenager."

I watched as the recognition washed over his face. "That was you. I... Wow. I... I hope you got the money I transferred to you."

I nodded. "Used it to join the police academy. Changed my whole life trajectory."

"Ironic."

"Quite," I agreed. "Still stealing paintings and selling them as your own?"

"On occasion," he admitted. "Still a cop?"

I shifted my weight. A valid question. One without an easy answer. "Depends on who you ask. If you ask my district, they'd say I went rogue months ago. If you ask me, I'd say 'yes.'"

My answer seemed to please him.

"So, you don't work for Connor?"

And there it was. The question he most wanted the answer to.

"Fuck no. I saved her from that monster."

That's when the girls broke apart. Both of them had tears in their eyes.

"I can't believe we found you. Are you okay? Are you hurt? How is your finger?" Amanda was asking as the tears streaked down her face.

"I'm okay," Kelli confirmed. "Holden had some Oxi so that's been helping with the pain. It hasn't turned black and fallen off yet, so I'm taking that as a good sign."

"Tell us what happened," Malcolm interjected. "How did you escape Connor?"

There was a lot to say, but I had to keep things short and sweet. We didn't want to linger here long. I formed the most succinct answer I could. "I was working undercover for one of Connor's colleagues. We were supposed to transfer Kelli to her new owner. They drugged her and put her in a fucking suitcase. A suitcase. Like she was nothing more than dirty laundry." I ground my back molars. "But I couldn't go through with it. I couldn't put her in the trunk of the car. When the other goon left to make a call, I took off with Kelli. I brought her here. It's a hideout for undercover cops who have blown their cover. And boy did I blow it. We thought you two might be Connor's men, honestly. They're looking for us. Guaranteed."

Malcolm nodded. "They're hunting us as well." He surveyed the sanctuary. "Has anyone been by since you got here?"

"Yeah. Two beat cops. So, only a matter of time before..."

Malcolm's eyebrows pulled together. "Before someone puts two and two together. Okay. That means we need to leave."

"It's too risky," I countered. "It's almost daylight. I'm not taking her out in the daylight."

Amanda and Kelli looked at each other, then back at us.

"True, but we have a window. We need to take it," Malcolm urged. "We have a car parked a few blocks away. From there, I'll get us transferred to my house in Florida—"

"More hiding?" Kelli asked.

"It's just until—" Malcolm tried.

"Until what?" Kelli's voice grew shaky. "Until Connor and every single one of his thugs is dead or in prison? Because that's never going to happen. None of us are going to be safe ever again. Isn't that what you're saying? That we're going to live our lives forever looking over our shoulder?"

I observed Malcolm's face. He'd wanted to believe the lie of eventual safety just as much as I did. The reality was that Kelli was right. We were never going to be safe. Not a single one of us.

KELLI

Three sets of eyes landed on me after I'd said the quiet part out loud. No one had a rebuttal. This was it. This would be our lives, forever in fear. Never knowing when one of us would be discovered. Amanda and I would likely be the higher priority as we could be re-caged and sold, but Malcolm and Holden... they would be killed. There was no room in Connor's world for people who stole his property. That was even if he condescended to let Amanda and I live. He might kill us for costing him his building. He'd probably take out his anger on us first, though. Anyway, you sliced it, the outcome wasn't good.

"Tell me again why we just can't go to the cops? I mean, we're fucked either way, aren't we?" Amanda asked.

"It's a gamble no matter which path we take," Malcolm said.

"And what are those paths?" Amanda was trying hard not to make all our options as grim as they were.

Malcolm let loose a deep sigh. "One, we hide in one of my safehouses for however long that means. And yes, that may mean long-term, but we'd be safe. We'd have protection. Provisions."

"And two?" The question came from Holden.

"We turn ourselves in. Trust that the entire system isn't bought and paid for."

"No. Take Kelli with you. Keep her safe." Holden's voice held firm. "I'll stay. I have unfinished business. I have a ring to take down. But priority one is keeping her out of that monster's hands."

"Agreed," Malcolm said.

"Hold up. You think you can make this choice for me?" I hissed. "You don't get to tell me what to do with my life. If I want to turn myself in, then I sure as fuck will."

"Kelli, don't be rash. You don't know how corrupt some of these stations are." His jaw visibly tightened. "I do. I've witnessed it firsthand. You don't know who to trust."

"Except you, right? I'm supposed to trust you? Is that it?" The wounded look that spread over Holden's face for the briefest of seconds made me feel horrible. But I quickly shoved that aside. Despite what we had done under the floorboards, I didn't know Holden. Not really. I didn't know what his motives were, or what his long game was, but I was long past people telling me what to do.

"He rescued you from Connor," Malcolm said gently. "I would hope that garners some level of trust."

"Try being locked in a cage and raped for a few months, and then, tell me how much you trust the actions of strange men."

Malcolm raised his hands in defeat.

"What do you think we should do?" Amanda asked. "I'm open to suggestions."

Gnawing on my bottom lip, I pondered the limited choices. "Let's start with what we know. Connor's business has gone up in smoke. Literally. He's on the run, God knows where. His men have likely gone underground, too, to keep off the radar. But that doesn't mean he doesn't still have connections. Those two cops sniffing around here yesterday... I tend to think Holden is right. That may get back to Connor, which means staying here isn't a viable option."

"So, you want us to walk out of here, with the sun approaching, where anyone might see us?" Holden challenged.

"Yes. But we do it in a strategic way."

"Which is?" Amanda asked. She at least seemed interested in my idea. The men, however, had looks of skepticism.

"We go in pairs. Me and Amanda together, then you and Malcolm," I said to Holden.

"What? No way."

"Out of the question," Malcolm chimed.

"Think about it," I said. "If someone is looking for us, they're looking for a man and a woman. Two women walking together shouldn't raise flags. Nor should two men, especially if you were holding hands. That would throw people off. No one is looking for a gay couple in this situation."

Malcolm and Holden exchanged disgusted looks. "You want me to frolic down the street holding hands with Malcolm?" Holden asked. His right eyebrow was pointed nearly to the sky.

"That's brilliant," Amanda agreed. "Plus, if they *are* looking for us, they're looking for a redhead and a blonde." She pointed to her now-black hair. "If we get you a hat..."

"Holden has one. I saw it in the stash of stuff."

Amanda reached out and took Malcolm's hand. "It could work."

"Slight hiccup, though. I'm only wearing a shirt. Won't that look suspicious?" I asked.

Amanda frowned. She knew I was right. That screamed sketchy. "Malcolm, give me your belt."

"Excuse me?"

"Your belt. We'll make this long shirt look like a dress with a belt."

"Oh, great idea," I said. "We'll just hope no one looks at my bare feet."

"No shoes in summer are totally a thing. Malcolm, belt?"

Malcolm gritted his teeth together but undid his belt and handed it over to me. "Let's entertain your plan for the moment. You don't think it will look strange that two sets of people come out of an abandoned church?"

"Not if we come in the way you did," Holden said. He was clearly thinking things through. "The back entrance is on a quiet street. We've been watching it. Plus, it's early morning. People are likely still sleeping. And we'll space out our exits. Where is your car?"

"Just a few blocks to the left of the church." Amanda seemed most eager for this plan to work.

"So... Holden and Malcolm head to the car, pull it closer to the sanctuary where you can monitor for any activity. We come out a few minutes later, hop in the car, and bing, bang, boom, We're out."

"And then what?" Malcolm asked.

I let free a slow breath. "Then we go to the FBI. Not local enforcement. I would like to think the Feds would be harder to buy out. They could offer us protection. Maybe set us up in witness protection or some shit. I don't know. But we can't stay here."

"It's not a bad plan, Malcolm." Amanda was doing her best to convince him.

"Except you're missing one small detail." Malcolm closed his eyes. "I'm also a wanted criminal. Going to the Feds means I'm in danger too."

"You could negotiate a plea deal," Holden said beside me. "Ask for immunity in exchange for your testimony. It's plausible. And even if it's not, your crimes wouldn't hold that large a prison sentence. It's not like they'd send you to ADX or anything for lifting some artwork. You might get off with fines and community service, especially in exchange for your testimony."

Malcolm seemed unsure. "I don't like leaving you two unprotected while we get to the car."

"I have a gun, Malcolm," Amanda reminded him. "And it would only be for a few minutes."

"And there is some pepper spray I can give Kelli," Holden offered. Looking at him, I realized he was taking my side. Tears welled in my eyes.

"So, we have a plan?" I looked around the room and saw three heads slowly nod.

"Perfect. Then let's get the hell out of this place."

CHAPTER SIXTEEN

MALCOLM

I didn't love any of this plan, but the weight of trying to hide four of us indefinitely at one of my safehouses loomed large. Sure, I could do it, but how sustainable would it be in the long term? My safehouses were meant to hold me over for a few months, at best. They weren't stocked to hold four people for months on end. And I'd already put Darcy and Camilla at risk helping me as much as they had. They deserved time to lay low and stay off Connor's radar. Perhaps going to the Feds was the only realistic option.

As much as I hated to admit it, Kelli was right. We were sitting ducks in the sanctuary. Especially if the cops had already scouted it. Realistically it would only be a matter of time before one of Connor's thugs was sent to check it out. We needed to be far away from this spot when they did.

Amanda's hand touched the gun still in the band of her pants. She was ready to go with Kelli. I didn't like this. It should be me protecting her.

"Wait fifteen minutes before following us to make sure nothing goes sour when we leave. If you hear anything, you abandon the plan." Holden looked to me as though to confirm the logic.

I nodded. We didn't want to be too close together, but any longer than that I would get antsy. Turning, I stared Amanda dead in the eyes. "I'll bring the car to the block just to the right of the sanctuary. We'll break right; you break left. You'll only need to walk to the end of the street. Bang a left and you'll see the SUV. It shouldn't take more than five minutes. We'll be able to watch you every step of the way."

"We'll be okay," Amanda assured me. "We've survived worse."

Pulling her into an embrace, I kissed the top of her head. "This is going to be over soon. I'm going to make this all go away." I felt her free hand wrap around my waist, holding me close.

"But not this, right? This will stay. Us?" Her voice was barely above a whisper.

Leaning away slightly so I could meet her eyes, I placed my hand under her chin to lock her in place. "This is forever. You're stuck with me."

"I'm okay with that." She kissed me then. I knew Holden and Kelli were likely watching with discomfort as I brushed my tongue against Amanda's, but I didn't care.

When we finally broke apart, Holden was by Kelli, instructing her on how to use the pepper spray.

"Holden, I appreciate the mansplaining, but I'm a woman. I know how to use pepper spray."

"Right. Sorry. I don't like leaving you unprotected."

Kelli frowned at him. "I'm not. I have Amanda. And if that fails, I can take him down with one hand." Holden raised a doubtful eyebrow. "My grasp on a man's balls is spot on. Wouldn't you agree?"

Holden's cheeks reddened, which told me everything I needed to know. He and Kelli had hooked up.

"Fifteen minutes," I repeated. "If you're not there, we're coming back, guns blazing."

"Keep your shirt on. This is going to work." Amanda gave me one last kiss before she stepped aside to let me pass.

Holden pulled Kelli to the side and whispered something to her that had her blushing right back. I shook my head. Is that how sappy Amanda and I looked?

A moment later, Holden was beside me, ready to rock.

"Follow me," I instructed. Holden nodded once as we headed for the door.

"Wait!" Kelli hissed.

Holden and I both turned to face her.

"You need to hold hands."

It was my turn to frown. "You were serious about that?"

"Absolutely. You want to be off their radar or not?"

Sighing deeply, I held out my hand to Holden. He rolled his eyes but took my hand. It felt all sorts of wrong. Just a few minutes. That's all we needed to keep up this ruse.

"Keep low until you leave," Holden warned. "Stay away from the windows."

It was good advice. I gave his hand a hard yank, anxious to get this over with. Shoving the door open, we stood in the doorframe momentarily as our eyes adjusted to the pre-dawn light. A fence in disrepair blocked our view, but once we cleared that we'd be out in the open. If Connor's men were lying in wait, this would be the chance for them to take their shot.

"You ready?" I asked him.

"My gun is in my holster. If they take me down, use it. Kill the bastards."

"Same." I lifted the back of my shirt to show my gun. We gave each other a mutual nod. There was comfort in knowing that we both had skin in the game.

I did my best to keep my pace brisk but not appear rushed. It was even harder not to look over my shoulder every two seconds to check for any signs of danger. Holden seemed to be struggling with the same thing. His hand was tense in mine. Like he was ready to pounce at any sign of trouble.

"The goon that was with you when you took Kelli," I asked, "where is he now?"

Holden shrugged while casually glancing toward the sanctuary. "Fuck if I know. I ditched him. He wasn't loyal to Connor, though. He was trying to pawn off Kelli as Amanda to another trafficker who goes by the name of Vincent. I guess Vincent wanted the pet Connor was obsessed with. Carlos was going to double-cross Connor and tell him Kelli was Amanda and get the reward for it. Kelli wasn't my assignment. Taking the ring down was. But I just couldn't... I couldn't let him take her."

"You did the right thing."

Holden nodded but I could tell he wasn't feeling great about it. After all, his decision had put us all in danger. Still, the right play. "So, Connor and this Vincent guy? They have beef. Like a turf war or something?"

He looked to his right, scanning the quiet neighborhood. The car was about a block away. So far, so good.

"It's a multi-billion-dollar industry. I'd be shocked if there wasn't beef. Clearly, Vincent wanted to hold Amanda over Connor's head for some reason. I'm not privy to why, though."

"Right. Do we have to worry about Vincent or his men coming after us? Would we be on their radar at all?"

"Depends on what Carlos did when he discovered I'd taken Kelli. Probably? I don't know. Carlos had a sick kid, so he was desperate for money. Desperate people do desperate things."

I glanced at our intertwined hands. "Yes, they do." I nodded once in the direction ahead of me. "There's the car."

A few more minutes and we'd be in the clear.

AMANDA

Kelli and I sat together, leaning against the door Malcolm and Holden left through a few minutes ago. Each of us seemed to be holding our breath, waiting for the sound of some sort of danger. So far, all I had heard was the chirps of birds waking up.

"How long has it been?" I asked Kelli, the nerves in my voice evident.

"You ask me that as though I have any way to tell the time. I don't even know what day of the week it is."

I glanced at Kelli, who was sitting on the ground beside me, hugging her knees. The pepper spray was grasped tightly in her good hand. "Sorry. I'm just nervous. It's going to be okay. This plan is going to work. Malcolm will keep us safe."

"How do you know that? Who is this guy? How do you know we can trust him?"

Right. She wouldn't have any idea who Malcolm was. And there wasn't a lot of time to catch her up. "It's a long story, but here's the long and short of it. I knew him in high school, weirdly enough. Before he got into the art-stealing scene. As fate would have it, Connor tried to sell me to Malcolm. He recognized me from back then because he had a massive crush on me. And well, instead of taking me for the two-week trial run as a pet that Connor proposed, Malcolm brought me to one of his safehouses in New Hampshire. And then, set me free."

"He stole you from Connor?" Kelli's eyes widened.

"I know. It didn't work."

"So that's why you were gone for so long. I thought he'd killed you, honestly. What happened then?" Kelli asked.

"Connor found us at Malcolm's safehouse. I still don't know how. But to keep Malcolm safe, I drugged him and hid him and basically performed the best acting of my life to convince Connor I was so happy he *saved* me from Malcolm." I shuddered at the memory. "It worked. Connor took me back to my cage and Malcolm, stubborn fool that he is, broke me out during the fire. He took me to a different hiding spot. That's when we got Holden's message about you. It took a lot of convincing for me to get him to risk coming here to find you after all the danger he'd put himself in because of me. But I had to risk it. If there was a chance to save you too..."

Kelli's eyes glossed over, and I could tell she was having a hard time holding it together.

"I'm glad you did. I don't know how much longer Holden and I would have been able to hide here undetected."

"Hiding under the floorboards was pretty genius."

Kelli nodded. "Yeah, that was his idea. It was a tight fit with both of us."

"Cozy," I said, watching her face carefully to see if she would give anything away about their relationship. She looked down at the ground. Busted. "So, you like him?"

"What's not to like? He's fucking hot." She laughed.

"You know what I mean," I chided.

Kelli shrugged. "We messed around a bit. But that doesn't mean anything. I mess around with a lot of guys." She tried to brush off her comment, but it was hard to deny from her expression that she wanted this time to mean something more.

"Believe me. I understand that. The things I did with Connor while I was caged..."

"Yeah," Kelli whispered.

"No. It's worse than that." I pinched my eyes closed.

"How do you mean? What did he do to you?"

"No, it wasn't like that. It was... God. I don't even know how to explain it. Like, I know Connor rapes the women he cages. He fucking made me watch him rape you. He's a literal monster." I sucked in a breath. "But somehow, I got it twisted in my mind that if I could get him to fall in love with me—desire me, he'd start to trust me and then I'd be able to find a way out. Get the rest of you out. Somewhere in that plan, it worked. He started to want sex with me. And I let him. It wasn't rape. I wanted him to fuck me. I enjoyed it. It was some of the best sex of my life. I know how gross that sounds. There's no justification. I'm just a fucked-up person, I guess."

"You were in a horrifying position and wanted to feel pleasure instead of pain. I don't see any shame in that," Kelli said plainly. "Hell, it's how I live my life. We gotta do whatever we can to suppress the trauma. It doesn't make you fucked up. It makes you a survivor."

Tears streamed down my face out of nowhere. "Thank you. You're probably one of the few who actually gets it. What we've been through... How are we supposed to get over that?"

"I don't think we will. I think there will always be reminders. Some are obvious." Kelli lifted her bandaged finger. "And some will be subtle. Internal. Like how neither of us may ever trust ourselves fully around men, now that we know what they're capable of."

"True. Although Malcolm is making a strong case for trust."

"You two serious then? I saw that kiss he planted on you earlier. You seemed to be into it," Kelli pointed out, fishing for more.

I nodded. "Yeah, we are serious. He loves me. And damn it all if I don't love him back. He's kind in a way I didn't know men could be. And the sex is amazing, so there's that."

Kelli chuckled. "Go after him. You deserve it."

I placed my palm on her knee. "You do too."

"Maybe someday. If we can get out of this situation first." Kelli rounded her shoulders. "It must have been enough time by now. You ready?"

"Beyond ready."

With that, we got up and prepared to make our break from the sanctuary.

CHAPTER SEVENTEEN

CONNOR

The text I'd gotten woke me from a dead sleep. One message changed everything.

> You won the bid. Transfer initial funds, and I'll send the address.

Carlos might be a backstabber, but he knew how transfers worked. You couldn't just transfer such large sums without drawing suspicion. Plus, it was time-consuming to do. Transfers of that size took several days. Carlos knew ten K was as much as could be done in a day, so that's what he was asking for. Little did he know, that was all he'd get out of me.

The transfer took a few minutes. As soon as it hit his account, the address came in.

> I expect the rest in weekly payments. Or I visit the Feds with what I know about you.

I smirked at the text. He wouldn't, but it was a nice bluff. He'd be dead before the week was out. I'd make sure of that.

With the address where Amanda might be hiding locked in my GPS, I packed up my gear and drove back over the border. She was a little over two hours away from me.

As I drove, I couldn't help but be curious about Vincent's bid for the information on Amanda. He must have lowballed it. Perhaps Vincent was hurting for funds more than he let on. It wouldn't surprise me. The condition he kept his women in couldn't make for good long-term pets. They'd either die in captivity or go mental on their owners. You could only sustain unhappy buyers for so long. Looked like Vincent would get what was coming to him—either by my hand or his own.

Glancing at the clock on the dash of my SUV, I pinpointed my arrival at the sanctuary to be just after dawn. Perfect. I could take down whoever was holding her while they were still sleeping and have her back in Vancouver by noon. Thankfully, Anthony was working the border patrol this week. He'd turn a blind eye to my plus one, once I slid him the wad of hundreds I set aside in the vehicle for such occasions. Then, finally, this shit show would be over. Vincent would take himself out with bad business practices, Carlos would be found and dealt with easily enough, and Malcolm... well, I could only assume that was who had Amanda. It would be the satisfaction of my life to sever his dick from his body. I'd give him two to the head just for my satisfaction. Then, I'd fuck Amanda right in front of his corpse so his spirit would know I always came back for what was mine.

My cock twitched at the thought of Amanda between my thighs. I was hard in seconds.

"Ah, fuck it." I switched on the cruise control and undid my pants. Better to tend to this distraction so my mind would be clear. Soon, my dick wouldn't have to settle for my hand. She would be mine. Ready to service me, whenever I wanted it. This time I wouldn't let her out of my site. I'd cage her properly, as I had been.

The thought of her re-caged, naked, and sitting on her knees ready to take me into her mouth had my hand working double time. Those lips. Those tits... I came in seconds. The fastest hand job I'd ever given myself. And it was all because of her. Even more evidence I was making the right call. In a matter of hours, she'd be mine.

CHAPTER EIGHTEEN

KELLI

Walking out of that church in the pre-dawn light was one of the scariest things I'd ever experienced. I had convinced myself that the second we cleared the fence, we'd end up with a bullet to the brain. When only the cool morning mist hit my face, I let loose a little laugh of hysteria.

"You good?" Amanda asked beside me.

"Yeah, just amazed that we aren't dead."

Amanda smiled beside me. "Yeah. I was holding my breath when Malcolm and Holden left. I kept waiting for a gunshot or something."

"Exactly."

We walked in silence for a bit as we darted our eyes around randomly, searching for any signs of danger. I held the pepper spray tightly in my hand as Amanda rested her hand on her hip, where the gun was hidden.

"Malcolm and Holden seem like solid guys, huh?" Amanda asked after a moment.

I nodded. "Totally not used to that."

"Agreed. Holden gives off good dude vibes. Think we can trust him?" Amanda was smart to question Holden. Our shared history of stranger danger was real.

"So far, he's not done anything creepy," I agreed. "I mean, he put his life in jeopardy to save someone he didn't know. That has to say something about a person, right?"

"Absolutely. And it doesn't hurt that he's not hard on the eyes," Amanda said, nudging my shoulder with hers.

"He's got a huge cock too." I smirked.

"I knew it! I knew you two screwed."

"No. We didn't screw. I just gave him a hand job while we were hiding under the floorboards."

"What?" Amanda shrieked.

I shrugged. "There wasn't much else to do, and I was laying on top of him, and wanted to thank him for saving me, I guess..."

"Jesus, do I get that? Malcolm kept refusing my advances to 'thank' him. I wore him down eventually. But good on you. Like you said before, no shame in trying to feel good in a horrible situation."

"He did feel good. I'll give him that." I was aware of how large I was grinning, but it couldn't be helped. He had a great cock. I shook my head. I shouldn't be thinking about our time under the floorboards. I needed to get my head back into the game. "We turn left at the end of this street, right?"

Amanda was doing her best to walk at a normal pace, but I could tell she was itching to get inside the car. "Yeah. Malcolm's SUV should be parked on the street. We hop in the back and then we should be good."

"Sounds too easy," I whispered.

She nodded. Far too easy compared to what we'd been through. Which might be why we both picked up our pace.

"So, you and Malcolm, are you two gonna, like, get married and have babies or something after this is all over?"

"Oh, wow. I hadn't really thought about that. I mean... maybe. One day? I'm not sure I'll ever be ready to have kids, nor probably should I, given all my trauma. What about you? You want kids?"

I bit my lip. "Want? Yes. But I can't have kids. I have POI."

"What's that?"

"Primary Ovary Insufficiency. It means that my ovaries stopped producing hormones and eggs when I was in my twenties. So, like I rarely get a period. But it also means, no baby-making ability. Probably for the best. Like you said, all that trauma would make me a horrible helicopter mom."

"Oh, my God, you're right. I'd never let them go in an elevator."

I laughed, despite how twisted that comment was.

We were nearly there. A few more feet until we hit the turn. Amanda and I seemed to hyper-focus on our steps. The time for small talk was over. Rounding the corner, I swear we both held our breath. Once we did, we both stopped walking.

"Where's the SUV?"

Amanda's question hung in the air, unanswered. A shiver ran up my spine. There were no black SUVs on the road. The only cars on the street were a white Jeep and a tan minivan, but outside of that, the street was bare.

"Maybe we didn't wait the full fifteen minutes?" I offered. "Maybe we didn't leave enough time for them to get here?"

"Maybe..." Amanda pointed. "Wait. There. It's right there."

Sure enough, a black SUV turned down the street just then. It stopped dead in the center of the road. The sky was just lightening enough to make things out. I glanced at Amanda, who nodded once. Together, we ran to either side of the SUV to crawl into the back seat. It was over. We were safe. Finally.

The second the doors shut; however, I realized our mistake. One sniff of the cologne wafting off the driver, and I knew whose car this was.

"Well, that was easy," Connor said. He turned around. He had a gun pointed at us.

Beside me, Amanda froze. I heard the locks engage and knew without even trying the door that we were trapped.

"Connor!" Amanda finally spoke. She almost sounded... relieved. "I knew you'd find us. I told Kelli, didn't I? I said 'Don't worry. Connor will find us. He'll bring us home.' And you did!"

What the hell was she saying? And why was she so excited to see him? Was this all a double cross or something?

Connor stared at me, and then down at my hand that was still clutching the pepper spray.

"I don't think you'll be needing that anymore." He nodded to the top of the side console, indicating I should leave the spray there.

I glanced at Amanda, who kept her smile locked in place. Her eyes pleaded with me to comply. Reluctantly, I placed the pepper spray down beside him. She followed suit and placed her gun beside the pepper spray. We were helpless now.

"Good girls."

My whole body shivered. "How did you find us? And what happened to the men holding us?" I asked. I was following Amanda's lead. She must have a plan.

"Excellent questions. But I think we'll save that conversation for another day. In the meantime, if you ladies wouldn't mind taking these." He reached beside him and grabbed a pill bottle. Roofies.

"Of course," Amanda took the bottle from Connor and dumped two pills into her hand. She handed one to me. "Here you go, Kelli." Amanda's tone seemed to beg me to cooperate.

What was she doing? Why was she being so compliant? Why wasn't she kicking, screaming, and trying to break the glass? That's when it hit me. That must be how she gained her power last time with Connor. That's why he was kinder to her than he had been with the rest of us. She'd found a way to outsmart him. To beat him at his own game. She'd managed to escape his grasp twice this way. I doubted she'd be successful a third time. But what was the alternative? If we tried to escape now, we'd be killed on the spot. As much as I hated to admit it, Amanda's plan would be the only logical one.

I reached out and took the pill. "Thank you, Master," I said. The words burned in my mouth, but I forced a smile, knowing I was about to go back to hell.

HOLDEN

With the car in sight, my muscles started to relax. We were almost in the clear. "So, when we get to the Feds, let me do the talking."

"Not a problem," Malcolm agreed. This is your area of expertise."

"It used to be... I don't know how welcome I'll be since I went rogue. They probably think I got lost in the underbelly or was killed."

He side-eyed me. "Why didn't you report in?"

A valid question. One he didn't need to know the real answer for. "I was being watched too closely. As a recent transfer from Vincent's operation to Connor's, I had to play it right. His crew is far more suspicious than Vincent's. Any wrong move could have blown my cover, so I just stayed in it, ya know?"

"You never felt tempted to stay? Reap the rewards of the hustle?"

My face contorted. "Fuck no. What Vincent and Connor do is ... unmentionable. I want to bring them down. To do that I need as much dirt on them as I could find. But now that we have you, Kelli, and Amanda—witnesses who can corroborate my findings—there might be a way to redeem my career while also bringing down two massive crime rings."

"Wouldn't that be nice?" Malcolm said. "Connor dead would be my first choice, but behind bars would be a close second."

Malcolm was about to cross the road to the car when I yanked his hand back.

"Wait."

"What is it?" he asked.

I took a deep inhalation. "You smell that?"

Beside me, Malcolm nodded. "Gas."

"You think someone messed with the fuel line?"

Malcolm ripped his hand from mine. "We've been clocked."

We stood there a moment in the pre-morning light, each scanning the area for the threat.

"What do we do?" I whispered.

"We abort. We need to get back to the sanctuary, keep the girls back inside, and get ready to be fired on." Malcolm reached behind him and placed his hand on his gun. I followed suit. Gone was any pretense of trying to lay low. We were in full defensive mode as we turned to run back to the sanctuary.

That was when the explosion came from behind us. I didn't need to turn around to see that the SUV was on fire. Which meant, someone *was* watching us, and they didn't want us to have an escape route. *Fuck. Fuck. Fuck.*

Our feet couldn't move fast enough to get back to the church. With every step, I waited for the sound of gunfire, or a scream, something to indicate that there were men inside. But all I could hear was the sounds of the fire behind us. Rescue crews would be onsite soon, which meant we had very little time to do anything.

Malcolm reached the back of the church first and nearly ripped the door off its hinge, trying to get inside. His gun was drawn, as was mine. We entered the building prepared for anything. Anything but what we found. An empty church.

"Kelli? Amanda? It's us. You can come out now." I made my way over to the hole I'd stayed in with Kelli, but it was empty. "They're not here."

Malcolm was scanning the pews, searching for them, when I saw something out of the one window that wasn't boarded up properly.

"There!" I shouted.

Malcolm followed where I pointed, and together, we ran to the window in time to see one black SUV, quite similar to Malcolm's, hauling ass out of the street we had told Kelli and Amanda to wait for us.

"Connor. He took them," Malcolm whispered. "He took them and blew up our only way to chase after him."

We both stood there, a wave of shock rolling through us.

Sirens began to wail in the distance. "We have to move. Now. Or we're going to risk being brought in."

Malcolm didn't budge. "Maybe that's what needs to happen."

"What? Have them bring us in?"

He nodded. "I don't know what to do from here, Holden. If Connor took them... I have no idea where he would go. I don't have resources like the Feds might. I mean, what other choice do we have?"

Looking out the window as the SUV gunned a left, I knew he was right. We'd played our last hand. We had no leads. No hunches. No information as to where they might be headed, or if he'd even let them live. Connor had pulled the rug out from under us.

"And if they arrest us?" I asked.

"If it means they might be able to find her, so be it."

"*Them*," I clarified. "If it means they can save *them*." At that moment, I realized that I, too, would be willing to go to prison if it meant Kelli could be saved. Maybe the information I had on Connor and Vincent might be enough to find out where he might take them. Or maybe this was where their story ended. Just like my sister. Gone forever in an instant.

CHAPTER NINETEEN

AMANDA

We'd been captured. Again. We'd put ourselves back inside his cage. We'd opened the door and let ourselves in. How stupid could someone be?

I could feel Kelli's eyes on me, ready to scream and do something stupid to get out of the situation we'd unknowingly entered. She was looking at me to do something, but there was nothing to be done. It was over. He'd finally caught up to us. There was an odd relief in knowing we didn't have to run anymore. A relief that was quickly replaced with acceptance. This was it.

We wouldn't get the chance to escape again. Connor won. We'd been outmaneuvered. All I could do now was do my best to lessen his anger at the two of us. The only way to do that was to appeal to his ego and his cock. So, I did the only thing I could do. I slid back into being the submissive he wanted.

I nodded at Kelli to take the pill. Her eyes shot me one last pleading glance before I saw her physically and mentally accepting our reality. Just like that, all fight left her. Her eyes glazed over, and her shoulders slumped, as her will to live seemed to evaporate into thin air. Kelli popped the pill into her mouth and leaned back in the chair, as though she wanted the feeling of nothingness to consume her. Her lids closed. She'd accepted the hand she'd been dealt. There was little else for either of us to do.

"Perfect timing," I said, trying to keep the shake out of my voice. "He was about to move us again." The roofie he'd given me was burning a hole in my hand. Everything in my body was screaming at me to toss the pill, get out of the car, and run as fast as I could, but the logical part of me knew that was futile. Even if I did manage to get free of the locked car, I'd make it two steps before he put a bullet in my brain. And I'd be leaving Kelli behind. But more than that, I could see something large on his lap. I couldn't be sure, but if I had to guess, it was some sort of detonation device. Was he going to blow up the church?

"Don't you worry about Malcolm. He's not going to be moving anything. Ever again," Connor said. He glanced over his shoulder, then pressed the button. I held in a scream as a huge explosion shook the car. My eyes darted to the church, but there was no fire. Smoke billowed from behind it, though. Black plumes filled the sky. Kelli didn't flinch. She was out cold.

"What was that?" I squeaked.

"Malcolm's ride. If I'm lucky, with him inside it. Either way, he won't be coming after you."

Malcolm. The SUV. That's what he blew up. *No... No, it can't be*. He was just saying that to try and get a reaction out of me. I held it together long enough to ask another question.

"Wow... that's... How did you know which vehicle was his?"

"An Aston Martin DBX in this neighborhood is a tad out of place. Not Malcolm's smartest play."

He did it. He'd killed Malcolm. Probably Holden too. The one good thing in this world Connor stole from me. How could I have been so careless as to drag him into my nightmare? I deserved anything Connor was going to dish out to me. And then some.

Connor shifted in his seat to look me dead in the eye. "Take your pill, Amanda."

And there it was. I was back in Hell. And I'd brought Kelli with me.

"Yes, Master."

Closing my eyes, I swallowed the pill dry.

If I'm honest, I was secretly hoping I wouldn't wake up. That he would have given me one too many pills, and I would overdose. I should have known I wasn't that lucky.

When I awoke, it was to the feeling of pain. My head throbbed. And there was something cold and heavy around my neck. Cracking a sluggish eyelid open, I fought to get my bearings. I felt nauseous. The room was spinning.

It was hard to focus on much for long. Everything felt fuzzy. Like waking after a bad hangover. Despite not being clear-headed, I reached up to try to understand what was around my neck.

As soon as my fingers touched it, I knew what it was. A chain. Around my neck and traveling down my body. My naked body. I shook my head to try to push the cobwebs away.

Even though I was groggy, there was no mistaking the situation. Connor had chained me to his bed, like a fucking dog.

"Good morning, sleepy head."

It took all my energy to turn my head. That's when I saw Connor coming into the room. He had a tray in his hands. "I brought you our traditional first breakfast. Remember? Toast, eggs, bacon, and of course, coffee."

"What time is it?" I asked, though that was the least of my questions, but it felt the safest to start with.

"Ten a.m."

"Man, I feel like I've been asleep for weeks." I rubbed my face, which still didn't feel quite right. Like waking from anesthesia. You're there, but you're not.

"Not quite that long." He set the food on the nightstand. "Although, it took a little time to clean up the loose ends. When I came to reclaim you, I didn't realize I'd have to deal with a secondary pet. I had to change my plans. Which meant I had to give you a few more doses to keep you under. I'm sure you have a huge headache now. Sorry about that, but it couldn't be helped. Offloading a pet takes time."

"Offloading... Did you kill her?" I blurted out before I could stop myself.

"And waste that revenue? No, she'll be delivered to her very grateful owner soon. He's eager to examine her healing finger so he can slice another part of her up another day. Men and their kinks. They never cease to amaze me."

Fuck. Kelli was still going to be sold to that butcher. All of this had been for nothing.

"And is this your kink?" I asked, holding up the chain around my neck.

"Having you naked and chained to my bed isn't a kink. It's how every pet should be treated. It's the best of both worlds. The pet has some freedom to get up and move around the premises, and the owner can feel safe that the pet won't run away because they are locked and secured to the master's set perimeters." Connor hummed in delight. "For now, your lead permits you to enter the bathroom. You can also sit in that chair next to the fireplace. It does not, however, allow you access to the windows or the doors, so there's no need to attempt it. Disobey me, Amanda, and your lead will be reduced. I'll let you lay in your own shit if you try anything funny. Are we understood?"

"Yes. Thank you, Master."

"That's a good girl. Now, let's get your breakfast sorted so we can christen this bed officially."

My mouth went dry. "Officially?"

He grinned wickedly. "I don't think you can technically count what I did to you while you were unconscious, but I just couldn't help myself. Your body was just lying there, begging to be fucked."

I smiled because that's what was expected of me. The tears pricked behind my eyes, but I refused to let them fall. He wanted me to be scared. And I was. But I wouldn't give him the satisfaction. This was my new reality. Forever chained to this man's bed. And not a sharp object in sight for me to end any of it.

CONNOR

I hadn't fucked her unconscious body. That was beyond even my morals, but I *was* curious how she would react to the statement. I still didn't trust her fully. I was trying to shake her into telling me the truth. But so far, she was being compliant. Too compliant. Hence the testing.

After all, I'd left her in a metal box in a burning building. I'd resigned her to an awful death. Then Malcolm managed to get up there and pull her free before the fire engulfed everything. Hard not to fall for that knight in shining armor routine, and yet, Amanda still seemed genuinely happy to be back with me, which put me on edge.

Eagerly, she licked the scrambled eggs from my fingers as I fed her. Even chained she was not to be trusted with utensils yet. Maybe one day.

"So, where are we?" Amanda asked as she finished her bacon.

I smiled and put the paper plate down. "This," I said as I gestured around, "is my childhood bedroom."

"Really?" She gasped.

Nodding, I stood up and walked over to the dresser. "I bought it when I sold my first pet. I contemplated burning it to the ground, considering all the horrible memories I had of this house growing up, but I decided that I'd keep the place, as it was, and one day... one day, I'd turn this into a real home. Settle down with the old ball and chain." I lifted her chain and grinned.

I tugged the chain to show her where it connected to the ceiling. "My mother had that hardware put in when I was twelve. Puberty, you see. I was rambunctious. I had many lessons still to be taught. The lead I've given you is yards more than my mother used to give me. I had three and a half steps past the bed. And a pot to piss in. Literally."

Her eyes widened.

The chain rattled in my hand. "My father would occasionally sneak me in food, but I never took it. I was afraid it was some trap set by my mother. Like she'd somehow see that I'd eaten when she hadn't given me permission. I would simply leave his offerings where he'd left them. Mother was proud I hadn't given into temptation and would reward me with another foot of lead." I laughed at the memory. Perhaps I could do the same with Amanda. Maybe one day she might even reach the dresser. Doubtful, but maybe, given time.

"I'm sorry she did that to you."

I glanced up. "Don't be. It was her lessons and her training that made me the man I am today. The world is made up of those who take what they want and those who obey. My job is to bring both of those people together. My childhood trauma, as some might call it, has made me a very wealthy man. But more importantly, it brought you here. To my bedroom. Some might call that fate."

"All roads lead to you," Amanda said with a seductive smile.

"You're damn right. Now, tell me everything that happened from the night of the fire until I found you. Leave nothing out."

For the next half hour or so, she told me about her time with Malcolm. She didn't remember being pulled from the building, but rather, waking in a strange place. Not dissimilar to how she found herself at present. Malcolm had gotten a tip that Kelli was being kept in the sanctuary, and the do-gooder that he was, he wanted to save her as well. That was where Holden came in. The transfer from Vincent, who'd done me dirty. I'd make sure he paid for that one day soon.

"Did you have sex with Malcolm?" I heard myself ask.

Amanda's eyes widened, betraying her.

"Depends on your meaning of sex," she said.

I pushed off the dresser and walked menacingly over to the

bed. "Did he insert his cock inside of your pussy?" My nostrils flared thinking of him with her.

"In that case, yes. He had sex with me, but what do you expect of weak men? But ask me why his time with me doesn't matter."

My teeth ground together. "Why?"

She slid off the bed and sank to her knees in front of me. "Because I *serve* only one master."

A second later her hands were on my cock, and I lost all sense of logic. I was hard in seconds when she took me out of my pants. A moment more, her mouth was around me, sucking me senselessly.

My hands dug into her now-dark hair as she moved her mouth up and down my length. I helped her along, rocking my hips into her waiting mouth. I wasn't proud of how fast I came, but her lips were magic against my dick. I was helpless around them.

"Fuck, woman! I've missed your mouth."

I pulled her up to stand and kissed her so deeply I could taste myself on her tongue. My hands roamed down her naked body, cupping her gorgeous ass. And just like that, I was hard again.

"Bend over. Ass in the air," I said, pointing to the bed.

Amanda quickly obeyed. Damn, her ass was fine.

I rubbed my hands around her cheeks, cupping and teasing her core. I inserted two fingers only to discover she was not ready.

"Amanda... why aren't you wet? You're always wet for me."

"Um..."

Was she not as turned on as I was? Was this an act?

"I need..."

"You need what?"

She looked over her shoulder at me. "I need you to smack my ass. Hard. Like you did before. Remember? After you showered me. On your bed?"

I raised an eyebrow. "You want to be spanked?"

"Yes, Master." There it was. There was that lust.

My hand came down hard and fast against her flesh, leaving a red mark.

"Ugh," she moaned. "Yes, again. Harder. Please."

Well, well, well. She liked the rough stuff. My cock twitched again as I complied with her wishes. I'd beat her black and blue if that got her off. And judging by her squirming, it may just come to that.

It took a total of five smacks before she was positively dripping. Finally, I could fuck her the way I'd been dreaming about. Everything this woman had put me through was going to be worth it.

CHAPTER TWENTY

KELLI

Everything was dark, cold, and eerily quiet. I blinked my eyes several times to make sense of where I was. At first, I thought I was still lying on top of Holden under the sanctuary's floorboards. My fingers stretched, trying to feel his shirt, but instead, they touched something metal and hard. Not Holden. That's when I felt my skin. No clothing. Why was I naked? That's when the memory of being captured by Connor came rushing back. My heart rate kicked into high gear. *Shit. Shit. Shit.*

I attempted to calm down to get my bearings. I froze and listened for several minutes to see if I could hear anyone. If someone was nearby, I didn't want to give away that I was awake. There was nothing to be heard, however, except the sound of my breathing, and an occasional drip from a faucet. *Hmm.* A faucet. I sniffed the air. It was musty. Like a basement. But whose basement?

Since I seemed to be alone, I decided to assess if there was any escape. First, I'd investigate the metal underneath me. My fingers traced the metal as it went under my legs. There was a pattern. Large metal squares. Weird. I tried to sit up, but I hit my head on something. Reaching up to feel what it was, it dawned on me. It was a crate. He had locked me inside a fucking dog crate.

I didn't even need to look to see if there was a lock on it. There would be. He'd recaptured me, caged me, and thrown me inside a basement. Was I to be punished? Sold? Or left here to die?

My body collapsed onto the floor of the crate as I stared into the darkness and shivered against the cold. There was no point in screaming. Connor would have made sure to put me in an area where no one would hear my cries. The cage would be inescapable, so I didn't waste energy trying to break a lock. All there was to do was close my eyes and hope they never opened again.

HOLDEN

"No, I told you, and the officer before you, that I don't know where they might have gone. Look, I've been here for hours. Are you seriously telling me that you don't have *any* information on two of the largest sex trafficking rings in the world?" I slammed my fist on the metal interrogation table at the FBI agency in a vain attempt to get some answers. Officer Crawford, a middle-aged white man, who clearly enjoyed a beer—or ten—after hours just looked at me, seemingly bored.

"I didn't say that," Crawford said. "I'm just awful curious about what you know. Seeing as how you were under deep cover with Vincent's crew, for what"—he picked up the file in front of him and flipped a few pages—"eleven months? Long time to spend undercover."

I understood what Crawford was implying without him even having to say it.

"Yeah, well it takes a long time to build the trust of these monsters."

"Still... what gets me, Agent Fontaine..." I flinched hearing my real name. I'd gone by Holden Knox for so long that it felt strange hearing my legal name again.

"What is it that gets you?" I knew my tone came off as

aggressive, but I was pissed. No one seemed to be doing anything. And with every second that ticked by, Kelli's life was in danger.

Crawford put down the file. "Your attitude for starters."

"Sorry. It's just... we're wasting time!"

"And how do I know you aren't wasting my time, Agent? You know how this works. We work with facts here. Not feelings. Now, you can either pull yourself together and answer my questions, or you can walk. Makes no never mind to me." Crawford placed his hands on his belly and leaned back in his chair.

I let out a deep sigh, rubbed my face, and composed myself. My hot head wasn't going to get us anywhere. Relenting, I gestured to him to proceed with his line of questioning.

"Good call." Crawford re-opened his file, glanced at it, then stared at me. "Tell me, what made you enter this gig in the first place? You were barely out of the force, and what? You just volunteered to be a part of a deeply risky assignment as green as you were? Hell, probably still are. What was the motive? You must have had skin in the game." His eyes narrowed. "Why take this assignment when you knew you'd be cut off from friends and family for God knows how long? What was in it for you, Fontaine? Did Vincent give you a cut of the action? Did he burn you, and now you come out of hiding to try and take him down? Is that it?"

"What? No. No way did I take payment from him."

"Outside of what he paid you for your efforts, that is?" Crawford raised an eyebrow.

"All those funds have been put into the account set up by my department as agreed when I started the assignment. Go on, check the statements. You'll see the only money I lived off was my fucking cop salary. Fuck you for assuming I'm dirty."

He shrugged. "What was your motivation then? Why put your neck on the line for such a high-stakes job? If you're as clean as you say and aren't in it for the money, what's in it for you?"

I could tell he wasn't about to let this line of questioning go. And until he got an answer that satisfied him, we'd be no closer to getting Kelli and Amanda to safety. As such, I threw caution to the wind and told him the truth.

"Vincent has my sister."

Crawford raised a white eyebrow. "Come again?"

"My sister, Shannon Fontaine."

He glanced at the file. "Says in here your sister ran away when she was seventeen."

Despite trying to stay relaxed, my whole body tensed. We were about to get into territory I didn't want to travel into. But given the situation, there didn't seem to be much of a choice. "That's what the cops from my town say, but I know the truth. She was taken."

"By whom?"

I looked him dead in the eye so he would know I was serious. "By Connor." I could see that had gotten Crawford's attention, so I went on. "Then, shortly thereafter, they sold her to Vincent. *That's* why I volunteered for this mission. It was about more than taking down a trafficking ring. I was trying to find my sister."

Crawford's face slipped from surprise to doubt. It was a bit of a wild story. I'm not sure I would have believed it either.

"And how do you know she was taken by Connor, specifically, and that she didn't just run off as teenagers do?"

"Because I was one of the men hired to move the women."

At that, Crawford leaned in and clicked his pen. "Go on."

I let out a heavy sigh. Tension pulled into my shoulders. This admission alone could get me locked up if Crawford saw fit. And maybe that was deserved. "It was years ago. I was a punk kid. Poor as shit. I hadn't found my way yet. I was involved in some less-than-legal work. Petty theft, that sort of thing. But then I got wind of this one-time gig that was gonna pay me a thousand bucks in cash. The details were vague. We'd be moving cargo from an SUV into a boxcar. My assumption was the cargo was going to be guns or drugs, honestly."

"What happened then?" His pen was scratching along his legal pad.

"So, me and some of my boys, like four of us, pull up to the location and see the train car in the middle of this vacant part of town. I didn't even know the railway still worked. Anyway, these big SUVs are all lined up. A few guys get out. Connor was one of them. He was giving the orders." I clenched my jaw at the memory of that piece of shit. "He told us to move the contents from the SUVs to the boxcar. The deal was better than advertised. A thousand bucks for *each* piece of cargo if we could get it done in ten minutes. Suddenly, we were all very eager and willing to help. Connor said that we couldn't say a word to anyone about what we were moving. If we did, he'd find out, and he'd come for us. We fucking believed him. The man was cold as ice. But none of us were gonna talk. We all needed the money."

"What was in the SUVs?"

"Women. Drugged and stacked, and zip-tied up inside the backs of these rigs like cattle. There were like ten of them crammed in there. And there were like eight or nine SUVs, all with bodies in them. It was revolting."

"And your sister was one of them?" Crawford asked.

I had to look away so he wouldn't see the tears mounting. The memory of her limp body... mascara running down her face, her freshly polished nails now chipped. She'd put up a fight until she was knocked out.

"I'm sorry. I know this is difficult to talk about," Crawford tried.

So much for hiding my emotion. Grinding my teeth, I sucked in a breath and turned back to him to tell him the details he wanted.

"My sister was near the bottom of the last car we unloaded. She was all dolled up because the last time I saw her, she was headed out to an open call for emerging models. Fucking scam. It was Connor. All these women tricked into believing they might have a chance at making something of their lives, only to be drugged and shipped off and sold to men to do God knows what with them."

Crawford scribbled some notes and then asked, "What happened when you discovered they had her?"

"I went ballistic. Tried to carry her on my shoulder and get the hell out of there. I was a scrawny kid back then, so I didn't get far before Connor shot me." I lifted my shirt and showed the bullet hole where it had hit me in the side. "It went straight through, but still, I went down. I think I might have passed out from the shock. They presumed I was dead. When I came to, it was morning, and there was no sign of anyone. All of my boys...they all left me for dead. A payday was more important, I guess."

"Did you report this to the police?"

"I did. They didn't believe me. Thought I was making up some bullshit story and probably was shot in a heist gone wrong, which given my past, wasn't that far of a stretch. So, I took matters into my own hands. If the cops wouldn't find her, then I'd get the skills I needed and find her myself. I had some cash stashed away from other gigs. That's when I enrolled in the academy."

His brows raised. "And did you? Find where they had taken your sister?"

"Eventually. It took a while, but I got a look at some of Vincent's books. He's old school. He keeps paper logs. Doesn't trust the internet for data storage. One day, he caught me looking at the transfer logs. Nearly broke my ribs for touching his records. But not before I saw Shannon's name. She'd been sold to a guy named Peter White. A dentist in Southern California."

"We'll look into that." More scratching in his notebook had my fists clench. "How did you walk yourself out of heat with Vincent?"

I flinched at the memory. "I told him I was just looking to jack off to the photos of the women. He couldn't find out the real motive. He would have shot me where I stood. But guys like Vincent understand men's kinks, so he let me live. But to pay him back for touching his shit, I was forced to do penance work. I worked under his thumb for a solid eight months before he finally trusted me. At that point, he sent me to go work with one of his guys, Carlos, to try and find a weakness in Connor's operation."

Crawford pulled his eyebrows together. "So, you were undercover, trying to take down Vincent's sex trading ring and got moved to another ring?"

"I know. It was nuts. But I figured the department would be happy to take either of them down. And Connor's ring would be the bigger deal, since he's mostly US-based and they would have more jurisdiction to prosecute."

He hummed his understanding. "And did you find dirt on Connor?"

"Carlos did. You see, Connor committed a cardinal sin of the human trafficking ring. He'd fallen for one of his pets. Connor now had a vulnerability that Vincent wanted to exploit. Vincent paid us to take his prized pet, Amanda, knowing Connor would pay a pretty penny to get her back. But the plan backfired." I cringed at the unintended pun. "Connor's building caught on fire the night we were going to take her. We got out with one of his other pets, Kelli, but Amanda was presumed dead. Carlos planned to lie to Vincent and say that Kelli was Amanda, then try to get the reward. After he got paid, he'd get out of dodge before the truth came out."

I rubbed my forehead, weary from it all. "That's when things fell to shit. I couldn't let one more woman be used and abused. I'd hit my limit, so, while Carlos was distracted, I took Kelli and hid out in the sanctuary, trying to figure out my next play."

He stopped scribbling to tap his pen against the pad. "Is this where Malcolm Luxx comes in?"

"Yes. He was the one able to get Amanda out of the burning building. I got him and Amanda to come to the sanctuary. I figured with four stories to corroborate what was going down with Connor, it would be enough to get some action going."

"It would have been." Crawford put down his pen. "Now, all we have are the words of two criminals. Not exactly a slam dunk for the DA."

"I know. But is there anything you can do? You must be tracking these guys, right? I can't be the only one on this case."

He steepled his fingers. "Are you, on the case? Your station claims you went rogue."

"That's only because there wasn't a safe time to check in, then the fire... and then the Kelli situation. Look, can you help them or not?"

At that, Crawford stood up. "Sit tight. I need to corroborate what you've told me."

"She could be sold off or killed any second now. We're wasting time—"

"Agent Fontaine, this is the Federal Bureau of Investigation. Here, we do things by the book, is that understood?"

I leaned back in my chair, deflated. "Yes, sir."

There was nothing to do now but wait and hope they were safe.

CHAPTER TWENTY-ONE

AMANDA

Asking Connor to spank me was a choice made from desperation. He wanted sex, and I wasn't ready for him as I had been in the past. How could I be? He had left me to die in a burning building, killed Malcolm, then chained me to a fucking bed. How was I supposed to be turned on by him?

And yet, I knew that if I didn't prove that I desired him, I would be punished. So, I pulled out the one thing that might help bring me there: trauma response. Being hit might trigger my body to behave. It wasn't desire, it was survival. If he could cause pain, perhaps the automatic toggle in my subconscious would flip, and then maybe, just maybe, I'd live to see tomorrow. Then again, did I *want* to see tomorrow, if this was what my future was going to be?

Connor did his part and brought the pain with each slap. My ass burned more from every blow. Tears stung in my eyes at how much it hurt. I let out a yelp and tried to make it sound like a moan. That's when Connor moved his hand from my ass and stuck two fingers abruptly inside of me.

"There's my wet girl," he said.

Thank God.

Connor tossed me onto the bed, face down. I was only vaguely aware of his touch. My brain worked overtime to focus on other things. The ornate carvings in the dresser, the pattern on the wallpaper. Anything at all so I wouldn't have to feel him inside me.

I tried to tune out the sounds of his breathing, the slap of his thighs against mine, the pain of his hands pulling my hair, and to think instead about the conversations I used to have with Malcolm when we were younger, sharing lunch together at school. The distractions were partially successful.

When it was finally over, he pulled out of me and smacked my ass again to remind me of the pain I would now be stuck in.

"Fuck, I've missed that," Connor said as he got off the bed to clean himself up with some tissues on his dresser. He tossed me the box. "I need to go tend to some business. Be a good girl."

He picked up his clothes from the floor and slid them back on as I lay on the bed, still recovering. A moment later, he was gone. Only then did I allow one single tear to fall.

Without wiping the tear away, I sat up on the bed and used the tissues to clean off as best I could. Since I had no idea when he'd be back or if I was being watched, I decided to play the part of caged plaything. At first, I just lay on the bed, thinking he was just outside the door, waiting to see if I'd try to escape. When it became clear he wasn't going to return, I tentatively got off the bed. I needed to see how far my lead gave me, and if there really was no hope for escape, but I had to do it in a way that wouldn't seem like I was trying to look for an escape. Just in case I was being watched.

Sliding off the bed, I heard the chains clattered around me, landing on the floor as I stood up. I tried to keep my composure relaxed and not panic. Connor was right about the lead. I could reach the toilet, and the sink, but not the shower. That must mean he planned to supervise those. Awesome. The windows were well out of reach, and the shades were drawn. I wouldn't be surprised if they were boarded up as well. I knew I'd never be allowed to check. The one chair I had access to was none other than a red wingback identical to the one he had in my cage. Twisted fuck. That was probably where he got the idea for the chairs: From his own goddamn childhood room. I was determined not to sit in that chair unless forced.

The floors were hardwood and cold against my bare feet. There was nothing warm or inviting about the room. During my inspection, I didn't note any cameras, or at least none that I could make out easily. In my last cage, it was obvious I was being watched. He wanted you to know that nothing you did was private. Here, though, there was nothing so clear, but cameras were small these days and could be hidden anywhere. So, I had to assume I was still being watched.

Walking back to the stripped bed, I sat. I wanted to break down and sob over the loss of Malcolm. Over Holden, whom I had just met. Over Kelli's fate and how it was sealed to a butcher. All lives destroyed because of me. The burden of that alone should have been enough to splinter my mind, but instead, all I felt was numb. Given the circumstances, it was a godsend.

Hours passed. Or maybe it was minutes. There was no way to tell the time. Another of his tactics. Deprive you of your sense of time. A good pet was one who was reliant on her master for everything. Food, shelter, clothing... Even knowing where they were in time and space.

I drifted in and out of sleep, getting up only to use the bathroom or splash a handful of water into my mouth. At some point, Connor must have come in while I was asleep to drop off food because when I woke there was something on the nightstand: a protein bar and a banana. While food was the last thing on my mind, I knew that he was unpredictable with his feeding schedule. Again, another way to mind fuck you. This might be all the food I would get for days.

Picking up the protein bar, I saw a note beneath it.

Welcome home.

Home. That was a joke. This room would never feel like my

home. The only place I ever felt remotely at home was when I was with Malcolm. Without thinking, I hurled the protein bar across the room in anger. It hit the wall, knocking off a picture frame which shattered to the floor well out of my reach. The broken glass I could have used as a weapon and the nutrients to keep me alive were both well out of my reach.

Fuck.

MALCOLM

After fourteen hours, a call to my lawyer, and several cups of cold coffee, Officer Crawford finally returned. He'd been going back and forth between Holden and me to see if our recollection of events was the same. I could only hope that Holden was being as truthful as I was; otherwise, this would end in disaster.

"Well, seems like your stories line up," Crawford said, sliding into the chair opposite me.

"Does that mean you'll look for them now?"

Crawford gave me a hard look, as though he were debating something. "That all depends."

"On?"

"What you're asking for." Crawford leaned across the table as he lifted one of his big eyebrows.

"I don't follow."

"What do you want in exchange for your testimony?"

Oh. "Nothing. Just Amanda brought back safely."

Crawford pushed back into his chair with a look of disbelief on his face. "I'm willing to guess your fancy attorney would disagree. Betting he's gonna ask for immunity from past crimes. As it is, based on your crime history, you're looking at twenty to thirty years, easy."

I ground my teeth together. "If it means saving her..."

"You love her that much, do ya?"

"I do. Please, find her."

Crawford was quiet for a moment as he pondered something. "If you can deliver Connor or Vincent, I could grant you immunity. It has to be one of the leaders. But if this ends up being a wild goose chase, you're looking at a long time behind bars."

"Understood."

He ran his finger along the folder he was carrying. He tapped it slowly a few times. "There is *one* lead we can follow up on. Might be a dead end."

"What is it?"

"Connor's childhood home. It was bought several years back at auction. Which isn't news. It's a nice house. What's interesting about the purchase is that it was bought by a shell company. And that shell company is owned by *another* offshore shell company, which is owned by, you guessed it, another shell company. Whoever bought it doesn't want it to be known that they bought it."

"Sounds like a move Connor would make."

He nodded. "After the sale, no one moved in. The property sat vacant. No one in or out for years. Then, you two show up with your story about Connor and how he might be somewhere in hiding. So, I had one of my agents swing by the area just to see. Suddenly, that vacant property now has the lights on. And there's a car parked in the drive with Washington plates. Might be nothing—"

"Or it might be where Connor took them."

"Exactly." He nodded to his file. "Warrant just came in, so we'll know in a few hours if it pans out or not."

This could be it. The place he was holding them. He would have needed a place to lay low. His building was burnt to a crisp. And after stealing Amanda and Kelli, he'd need to regroup. Then again, going to his childhood home felt a little too much like a trap. Connor was slippery. Was he counting on the police to raid the place and then open fire? If this was a trap, I wouldn't be there to save Amanda.

Crawford stood and went to the door. "Well, you coming or not?"

I cocked my head. "I can go with you?"

"If you're right, and he's got them there, I'll need you to identify the captured women... or their bodies."

I pushed out of the chair so hard that it fell behind me. I would not be identifying Amanda's body. Not today.

CHAPTER TWENTY-TWO

KELLI

Hours passed. With each minute that ticked on, I could feel the numbing effects of the roofie wearing off, and I fought against it. I didn't want to be fully aware of my situation. I wanted to live in the fog of the in-between.

Eventually, I tried to sit up, but it was useless. There was no space to move more than an inch or two from where I was. Nothing had changed since the last time I'd opened my eyes. I was still naked and locked in the cage, but now I was alert enough to make out that there was a small shaft of light coming in from a boarded-up window in the corner. It wasn't much, but it was enough to help me get my bearings. I was definitely in a basement.

To my left was a stairwell that led up to the rest of the house. Stairs I'd never be granted access to. There were four narrow basement windows that I could probably squeeze out of if I could get myself up that high. But again, I wasn't going to be allowed out of this cage to attempt it. Shelving lined the sides of each wall, but it was too dark to make out what was on them. Knowing Connor, it might be dead bodies. Was this where he took pets that misbehaved? Did he leave them here in cages to starve to death? Good. Better to be dead than sold off to that butcher. At least there would be an end to my suffering.

That was when I heard noises from above. Someone was whistling. My breath stopped. Then, the sound of a door unlocking drew my attention. More light spilled into the basement. Squinting against the sudden brightness, I focused on the staircase and saw a pair of legs descending from the light.

Connor.

"Ah, good morning. I see you survived the night. That's good. Not every pet does well on such high doses. I'll be sure to pass that tolerance level on to your new owner. He'll be here to collect you soon, so I thought we best clean you up."

So, not left to die. Figured. "Where are we?" I asked. It was useless to plead for help. I'd get none from Connor, but maybe he'd let some other stuff slip.

"You're at a temporary foster home. But don't be sad. Your new owner is so thrilled you were found safe and sound."

"You mean butcher." Connor smiled as he glanced down at the finger that had been severed and sewn back together by my new *owner.*

"Yes, well, boys and their toys." Connor sighed. "His tastes are a bit gruesome for my liking, but we can't help what gets us off, I suppose."

"What gets you off? Throwing women into cages?" I was surprised by how brazen I was being, talking back like this, but since there were no other girls to punish for my insubordination, and I didn't care if he killed me, I had little to lose.

"Someone has gotten mouthy in her time away," he tsked. "I envy your new master training that bite out of you. Maybe he'll need to take your tongue."

I swallowed down the fear at the thought. Note to self, don't say a fucking thing to the new master. Dying was one thing. Being mutilated was another.

"Come, we have to get you groomed before your master arrives." He knelt and reached for the lock on the cage. "Kelli, if you make any attempt to hurt me, or run, or do anything other than what I tell you, I will not hesitate to kill you and Amanda. Sale be damned. A disobedient pet is not worth keeping alive. Is that understood?"

Amanda. Was Amanda here? Was she caged too? *Fuck*. Now I had to behave because he would hurt her if I stepped out of line. Swallowing, I nodded. "Yes, Master."

Robotically, I crawled out of the cage with great discomfort after being crammed inside there for so long. I had no sooner stood up than he grabbed my arm and led me over to a corner of the basement. He flipped on a light switch, and suddenly, I could make out more of the room. The area where he was leading me was some sort of makeshift shower. Embedded in the concrete was a two-foot by four-foot metal drainage grate. Above that, a shower head.

"Mother used to put my kennel here when I was a child so that when I would eventually have to use the bathroom, she wouldn't have to clean me off. She'd just turn on the shower until the water ran clear." He let out a small exhalation. "Fun fact: She did *not* use the hot water."

He reached up and turned on the tap. The sound echoed off the concrete walls, causing my skin turned to gooseflesh.

"When Mother had this installed, she told the workers she wanted something to hose off the dog because she didn't want the filthy things in her tub." Connor shook his head. "We never had any dogs. This was strictly for me and my training. No matter. Now, I can use it on my pets. An unexpected gift from my mother."

He shoved me under the water, which was so hot it was almost scalding. A second later, my hand was jerked upright, and I was quickly handcuffed to a hook on the wall.

"They do this with dogs, too, when they're groomed. Locking them in place while bathing them keeps the groomer safe. Some pets need muzzles, which I have, as well, if you try and bite."

I didn't doubt that for a second.

Once I was properly secured, he went over to a cabinet to get the supplies he needed.

"Let's see. What sort of groom does your owner want?" Connor glanced at a piece of paper. "Ah, yes. 'Legs and pits shaved, but the bush to be left lush.' I prefer it that way myself," he said, grinning at my crotch. He went back to his notes. "Let's see, 'nails to be left bare, and hair down and natural.' Very Gweneth Paltrow." He grinned, likely remembering the name of Gwen that he'd given me. "Ah, yes, attire: 'Simple white sundress. No undergarments.' Ha, kinky." Connor stared at my body. "I think I have something in here that will do just fine."

I closed my eyes as I grappled with my fate. I was to be dressed up and be used as someone's sex doll. If I had tears left to cry, I would have released them, but instead, I just stood silent, wishing I were dead. I might soon get my wish.

CONNOR

Once Kelli was shipped off to her new owner, I would have enough funds to keep me liquid for a few months as I figured out my next play. In time, I'd have to eventually move Amanda to Vancouver once things calmed down. A job that would easily be achieved with the right bribery at the border. Two women, however, would have been pushing my luck, so I had to offload Kelli.

Ultimately, this was a good thing. The unexpected discovery of two pets at the sanctuary may have altered my plans, but it also proved to line my pockets. With an immediate cash flow, I'd be able to take some time to tie up loose ends and then deal with the ramifications of how Vincent double-crossed me. Of course, I'd hire a goon to take out Carlos, after I'd screwed Amanda a few dozen times over. Priorities.

When Kelli was groomed and dressed, I put the ankle monitor

on her. The doctor would replace it with a collar he had custom ordered, but this was temporary to aid in the transportation. Not that I anticipated any issues. Kelli had been quite compliant, despite her pathetic attempts at rebellion.

Just as I was lacing up her last sandal, my cell went off. It was the burner phone I'd set up for this transaction alone so there was only one person it could be.

"Doctor Wallace, good to hear from you. I've got your pet all groomed and ready for pick up."

A hiss like static reverberated over the line. "About that. I'm going to be late. Surgery ran over."

"Ah, yes, well, that can't be helped, I suppose. How late? I do have other engagements to tend to."

There was a pause on the line as he adjusted the phone. "I'll be there in about an hour. That work?"

"Yes, that works fine. Oh, I forgot to ask, do you want an anal plug in, or would you prefer her ass tight?"

Another pause. I could tell my question had thrown him for a kink loop. Both options could leave one salivating.

"Leave it out," he said quietly.

"Tight it is. See you soon."

I hung up and tucked the phone into my pocket. "Lucky you, no plug. Though, you know I much prefer the real thing to a plug. I feel it trains muscles better. Wouldn't you agree?"

She nodded.

Good girl. She was accepting her new reality. Life as a pet to that twisted fuck certainly wouldn't be ideal, but it was still better than some owners I'd sold to.

I picked up the butt plug. "Maybe I'll bring it upstairs to Amanda. Pain does seem to be her thing."

"Amanda is in the house too?" Kelli asked.

Fuck. I shouldn't have let that slip about Amanda. I drew my hand back and smacked her across the breast. "I did not permit you to speak."

Kelli held back the pain I'd caused her by biting her lip. She nodded her understanding. Who I had with me was none of her concern. All that mattered was that in one hour, I'd be free of Kelli and finally able to spend all my time fucking Amanda's brains out. It was a good day to be me.

CHAPTER TWENTY-THREE

AMANDA

The irony of my situation was not lost on me. The two things in the room that could be the most beneficial to me: food and a possible weapon from the shattered glass were just beyond the reach of the chains. That didn't mean I still wouldn't try to get them. Hopping off the bed, I stretched out my hand, willing my fingers to grow longer to reach either item. The chain around my neck held me back from the final foot that I needed. Foot... I glanced down at my bare foot. Hmmm. My neck was chained, but not my legs. If I were to lie down, I bet I could reach one or both with my toes.

Pulling the chain as far as I could without cutting off air, I lay on the ground and swung my legs toward the fallen glass, trying not to slice myself open in the retrieval. The protein bar was surprisingly easy to capture as it was closer and not sharp, but the glass shards proved more difficult. Each time I tried, I could feel the slight bite of the glass warning me to ease off.

Trying a new tactic, I aimed for the fallen frame. Surely there would be some glass still inside it. A wooden frame would be easier to retrieve with bare feet than a single shard anyway.

Shifting my body across the floor to get closer to the fallen frame, I paused. I heard running water. *Fuck*. Connor hadn't left.

He was still here. Probably taking a shower. Which meant he could return at any second. Frantic, I pushed out my feet to reach for the frame. After several failed attempts, my big toe finally caught the corner of the wood, and I managed to slide it across the floor.

Panting, I pushed against the bed so the chain around my neck wasn't so tight and pulled the prize to me: a family portrait. Connor with his mother and father. All dressed up to the nines. Connor was maybe six or seven in the photo. His father had a full head of hair and didn't resemble the drunk man he'd morphed into later in life. The mother looked airbrushed to perfection. But there was something in her eyes that showed no life. Just coldness. That was when I noticed her hands on her son's shoulder. A typical pose of a mother and son, but her fingers were clearly digging deep into Connor's lapels to lock him in place. The matching vacant smile Connor wore betrayed her cruelty.

I almost felt sorry for him. Almost. But we all had choices in life. We'd all had fucked up things happen to us. But it was the choices we made that defined us. And Connor had chosen to continue her legacy of abuse. I was choosing to break it.

As though the universe was conspiring with me, I saw my chance. Tucked safely inside the corner of the frame was a large, knife-shaped shard of glass. I'd get one shot at this. And one alone. I wasn't stupid. Killing Connor would be sealing my fate as I was chained and wouldn't be able to escape if he were dead. I would starve if he died. But if that was how this cycle ended, then that was how it ended. After all, what else did I have to live for?

KELLI

Connor seemed frustrated when he got off the phone. He had me sit on a box and ordered me not to move while he switched between different phones, scrolling messages. I must have been sitting there, motionless, for a good forty minutes before I decided to ask a question.

"What should I call my new master?" Besides butcher?

"Whatever the fuck he tells you to call him," Connor said, narrowing his eyes at me. "What? You don't honestly think I'd give up my client's real name, do you?"

"Why would it matter? I'm going to be locked away. Who would I tell? Besides, it's not like it would be hard to figure out. I can't imagine there are a ton of hand surgeons in the Seattle area."

That comment earned me a slap across the face. I should have expected it, but normally he left the face alone. A blow to the gut would have been more on par with Connor's actions. But he seemed frazzled.

"I never said he lived in the area. I have the means to fly in prospective buyers any time I want. Talk again and it will be the last time you speak, ever. Understood?"

I doubted he would risk harming an asset so close to a sale, but I decided I wouldn't push my luck.

"Your new owner will be here soon. Pay attention because I will not repeat myself. When he arrives, we will meet him in the driveway. Once he has paid me, I will release you into his care. When I let go of you, you officially become his property and must obey his every command. If you disobey him in any way, swift action will be taken. If he is dissatisfied with your behavior, he can return you to me for additional training. Trust me, Kelli, you do not want to be sent back to me."

I merely nodded my understanding.

"I know it will be tempting to try to run once we are outside, but don't forget, you have an ankle monitor on. I am tracking your every step. Even once you make it to your new place, your owner will have you collared. If you are someplace you're not supposed to be, I will know it, and I *will* hunt you down and kill you. Pets who run, get euthanized. Are we quite clear?"

Another nod.

Connor grunted before he went over to one of the shelves

and took a gray case down. After popping the lid, he removed the gun that was inside. He loaded it and tucked the gun into the back of his pants. It was a scare-tactic for sure. A way to remind me how much control he would have over the transfer. Part of me wanted to run so he *would* kill me. At least then I wouldn't have to deal with the fear of the unknown anymore. But one day, when I had enough courage, I would run, and I would accept the bullet to the brain happily. I just wasn't there, yet.

His phone beeped then. He pulled it out and nodded. "Okay, he'll be here in a few minutes. Let's get into position."

He grabbed me by the back of the hair, yanking me like a dog who'd pissed on the carpet, and dragged me up the stairs. The stairs opened into the kitchen. There were bulk packages on the countertop covered with boxes of protein bars, water bottles, and paper goods. The smell of bacon lingered, and a dirty pan rested on the stove. I didn't see much more than that before he brought me outside. The air was brisk, causing me to shiver. The sun was up, but it was still chilly, which told me it must be morning.

"The cool air is bringing out your nips. Delightful. I'm sure he'll love that."

I stood beside him, shivering, not only from the cold but from what was to come. Woods surrounded us. No neighbors to see what was happening and call the police. Connor was too smart for that. He was right. There was nowhere to run to. Even free of the cage, I was still trapped.

Just then a car pulled into the driveway. A red sedan. Very suburban dad vibes. Not the sort of car you'd expect from a kink monster like him. In the front seat was a man with dark curly hair and glasses. I recognized him at once as the same man who'd stitched my finger back on. My eyes darted to the scar on my hand. How many more scars would he give me?

"There he is," Connor said. "Smile, Kelli, or should I say, 'Gwen.' Your new life is about to begin. Aren't you excited? I just love adoption days."

I did my best to put on a smile, but I was shaking so badly my teeth were rattling.

The car came to a stop about twenty feet away from us. The man got out of the car tentatively, like he was nervous.

“Sorry, I’m late.”

“No bother. So glad to see you again. This time under less bloody circumstances.” Connor started to walk toward him, but the man lifted his hands.

“I’ll come to you if you don’t mind. I have patient records in my car. Confidential.”

Connor raised an eyebrow. “Of course. Whatever makes you more comfortable. Doctor, this is Gwen. Gwen, this is your new master. What would you like her to address you as?”

“Um, ah, how do you mean?” He twitched his hands.

“Would you like her to call you Master? Doctor? Some other phrase?”

“Uh, um, Mike is fine for now.”

“Mike.” There was something about the way Connor said his name that told me, “Mike” was not his real name. “Well, go on, Gwen, say hello to Mike.”

Dropping to my knees, I did as I was trained to do whenever I was to greet my new master.

“Look at that,” Connor said. “Ready to serve you already. If you want to pull your dick out and try her out, I won’t object.”

“That won’t be necessary. Just get in the car. Back seat. Passenger’s side,” the doctor said.

Connor shook his head at me. “Not so fast, *Mike*. There is the little matter of payment?”

“Oh. Right. Of course.” He dug into his suit jacket and pulled out a crumpled manila envelope. “It’s all there. As discussed.”

This was it. The last moments before a new hell began. I closed my eyes, rocks cutting into my bare knees as I waited for Connor to take his money and sell me off. After all the months of being caged, raped, hit, starved, and mutilated. What more could I possibly live through?

With my eyes closed, I clung to one memory: Holden's arms around me, holding all my broken pieces together. Once I opened my eyes, I knew that I'd have to let those memories go. There would be no holding me together anymore. I was about to be taken apart, one body part at a time.

Unfortunately, I wasn't granted the time for Connor to count the cash. "I trust it is, Mike. I know where you live if it's not," he warned. "But I have to say, you seem nervous."

"Mike" stood up a little taller. "You might be used to sex trafficking deals, but I'm not."

Connor clicked his tongue at him. "Sex trafficking is such an ugly term. I'm merely selling you guaranteed loyal companionship. A pet. What you choose to do with the bitch is entirely up to you."

"Yes, well, whatever you want to call it, it's not exactly legal, so sue me if I'm a bit nervous." The doctor's eyes darted around the woods, as though expecting the police to burst out and make a bust. There would be no rescue mission. No one knew we were here. And even if they did, why would they care about two woman no one had reported missing?

"Well, there is nothing to worry about. As you can see, I'm quite remote out here. Just us and the birds. And maybe a bear or two."

"Is that it then? Is the deal done? Can we go?"

Connor laughed. "Someone is anxious to play with their new toy. I don't blame you. She's an excellent ride." He kicked me then with his foot. "Get up and get in the car."

Opening my eyes to my new reality, I stood.

"I'll reach out to you in a week, and see how things are going," Connor said, more as a reminder to me than anything.

I wasn't going to run. Yet. But I would. Soon. Or I'd die on his operating table. One of the two.

CHAPTER TWENTY-FOUR

KELLI

I didn't know how my legs were propelling me forward. Or how my breath remained so calm. Survival mode must have engaged deep inside of me to move my body closer to the car. My eyes had glassed over with tears so badly I could only make out the rough shape of where I was going. The lump in my throat threatened to deprive me of air. My brain shouted at me to run, take my chances, and escape while I could. But my gut understood the reality. This was it. The end of one horror story and the start of a new one.

Reaching the car, I opened the back door as instructed. I climbed inside, shut the door, and closed my eyes, letting the tears fall freely while they could. Once the monster got in the car, I would have to become devoid of all emotion. But for now, I allowed myself one small moment to mourn the person I was. *Goodbye, Kelli.*

That was when I felt something touch my ankle.

My throat was too tight to scream; so instead, my eyes flew open to see what touched me. Yet, because of the tears, all I could see was the dark shape of something on the floor. Someone else was in the car.

"Don't make a sound. Keep looking forward."

That voice. I knew that voice.

"Holden?" I whispered. I wiped the tears from my eyes to confirm what my ears told me. My vision cleared, and my heart skipped. It was him. He was here. How... How was that possible?

He lifted his finger to his lips and had his weapon drawn. He gestured to where my new owner was still talking with Connor.

Hope lifted in my chest as my heart beat a mile a minute. Holden was here. Rescuing me. It didn't compute.

"Just act normal. Keep your eyes ahead," Holden whispered. "This is a sting."

A quick nod told him I understood. I didn't take my eyes off Connor and the doctor talking in the distance. What if Connor got close enough to see Holden in the car?

"Is Amanda inside?" Holden asked. "Blink once for 'no' and twice for 'yes.'"

I blinked twice. Where in the house, I had no idea, but Connor had let that nugget slip.

Glancing back to Connor, I felt my hands ball into fists. "He's coming," I whispered, trying not to move my lips. My legs started to shake in fear.

Holden shifted his weight and raised his gun toward the passenger's side with one hand. With his other, he wrapped his fingers around my calf to help settle my fears. Calm washed over me.

The driver's side door opened, and the doctor got in.

"Don't say a word, Doc," Holden instructed. "Put your seatbelt on, start the car, and back out slowly. Take a left once you're on the main road and drive until you see the police barricade. No funny moves or this ends here and now. Then, we tell your wife and your hospital everything you did and were planning on doing to this poor woman back here."

The doctor did as he was told, and soon we were backing out. I could see the satisfied grin on Connor's face, even as we backed away. He thought he'd made a successful sale. It was all I could do not to stick him the finger, but I restrained myself.

"The barricade is about a mile down this road."

Behind me, I heard a noise, and I jumped.

"Relax. Two more officers are in the trunk. We have five more in the woods. You honestly don't think they'd trust me to do this alone, do you?"

Now that we were out of Connor's watchful eye, I stared down at Holden, who was still ducked low.

"How... How are you here? How did you find us? I don't even know where we are."

"It's a long story, but basically, we went to the Feds. Just like you wanted us to. They cut a deal with the doctor to bring you two in safely, and hopefully, take down Connor's ring in the meantime."

"You mean, this nightmare might finally be over?" I didn't trust the words.

"In theory, this will be all over in the next few hours. You'll be able to go home."

I glanced out the window. That should have brought me comfort, but it didn't.

"I don't have a home. I was taken while looking for an apartment, remember? I have no family. No money. No job. What the hell am I supposed to do now?"

Holden's face fell as he took in my words. "You'll stay with me then. I have a place. It's small, and probably dusty as Hell because I haven't been there in almost a year, but I'll make sure you are safe."

"You don't have to do that. I'm not a charity case." I rubbed my face. "There must be homeless shelters or something where I can go until I get back on my feet."

Holden squeezed my leg. "I'm not letting you go to a shelter. I'm not letting you out of my sight. You're coming home with me, and that's final."

"Yes, Master." I flinched. "Sorry, force of habit. What I meant to say was thank you. Just for a few days. Until I figure something out."

"Stay as long as you want."

I liked the sound of that, but I didn't want to admit it, so I changed the subject. "You said your place is small. Is it bigger than under the floorboards?"

Holden laughed. "Yes. It's bigger than that hole in the ground."

"Pity. I rather liked being in there with you."

His hand moved gently up and down my calf. "I did too."

"Okay," the doctor said. "The barricade is up ahead. What do I do?"

At that, Holden sat up and helped guide him through the barricade. The car stopped, and then a rush of things happened all at once. The doctor was removed from the car, handcuffed, and placed into a cop car.

"It's him. He's there. He's got Amanda inside," Holden said to an older man with white hair. That man turned and talked to officers beside him while Holden brought me over to a waiting ambulance to get checked over. And then, a second later, five cop cars sped down the road to Connor's without their sirens to catch a monster. I could only pray that when they arrived, Amanda wouldn't be found dead.

AMANDA

Outside, I could hear a car driving up, and the sound of Connor's voice. Their conversation was muffled, but two men were talking. There were no raised voices or guns going off, so whoever was here was someone Connor expected. Was it reinforcements? If so, that meant my escape was even less likely.

Nausea swept through me. Sweat began to form at my temples, and I knew I was about to hurl up the remaining roofies in my system. Scrambling, I tossed the glass shard on the bed, then ran for the bathroom. My knees hit the floor just as everything he'd fed me for breakfast came back up. Once my stomach was empty, I lay on the cool tile floor, waiting for the room to stop spinning.

"Amanda," Connor sang from somewhere in the house. "I've got good news."

I could hear him coming up the stairs. *The glass shard*. I had to hide that before he saw it.

Pushing myself up to stand, I wobbled a bit as I regained my balance. The heavy chain behind me dragging onto the floor made my advance to the bed seem to take forever.

As the bed had no sheets or anything to cover the glass, there was only one place for me to hide it before he came inside: behind my back. I held the glass in my hand as tightly as I could without slicing my palm and sat on the edge of the bed like a good girl.

A moment later, a grinning Connor came into the room. "Looky what I have," he said as he waved a manila envelope in the air. "I just sold Kelli, so this chunk of change will be enough to let us live here unbothered for several months."

My heart sank. Kelli was sold.

Connor opened the envelope then, and without warning, there was a loud pop, and a puff of red filled the air. It took several seconds for Connor to figure out what had happened.

"That mother fucker," Connor hissed. "He set me up."

"What? Who? What is that all over your hands? Is that blood?"

Connor's hands were covered in red.

"It's bank dye. That means the fucking doctor went to the cops. He played me."

Connor tossed the ruined money to the ground, went to the window, and pulled back the curtains. It wasn't boarded at all. Just a normal glass window. That's how confident he was I wouldn't escape. Then, I heard the sound of multiple cars coming into the driveway.

"Fuck. It's a raid."

Hope filled my chest.

Connor looked at me briefly and then glanced at the door. "Sorry to leave you naked and caged again my pet, but there's no time."

He headed for the door, paused, then turned back to kiss me.

"I'll find you again. Don't worry," he whispered in my ear. "I'll always come for you."

I believed him. And there was no way I was going to let that happen. Using every bit of strength I had, I pulled the shard out from behind my back and jabbed it straight into his side, trying to hit any organ that would take him down.

Connor stumbled backward as his eyes went to the glass inside him and then back to me. The look of betrayal on his face almost made me feel bad.

"That was for Kelli," I hissed.

"You backstabbing bitch." He yanked the glass from his side. The one thing you were not supposed to do when impaled, according to all the crime shows I've watched. Removing the object made you bleed out faster. The way he stumbled as he removed it had me believing those shows were right. He was getting paler by the second.

He stumbled toward me, blood gushing out of his side, the bloody weapon now held out at me. I scrambled onto the bed to put as much distance between us as I could. He was having difficulty walking, so I knew he was in pain.

A loud crash echoed below us, and then lots of shouting as people entered the building. Connor's eyes darted from the door to me, as though assessing what was more important, ending my life or saving his.

Dropping the glass, he rushed to the window. He threw it open and had one leg out of the window when about ten men rushed into the bedroom. A flurry of shouting and warnings overtook everything, and before I even knew what was happening, an officer with riot gear was pulling me away from danger as the rest of the team assembled on Connor. They had him on the ground and in cuffs before I could even process it.

Five men had their knees on Connor's back as they secured his cuffs. A cascade of shouting filled the air. A moment later, a medic was allowed into the room.

"Oh, no, you twisted bastard," the medic said. "You're not

gonna bleed out. You're going to serve your time for what you've done."

I closed my eyes, hoping against hope that the medic wouldn't be able to save him. I didn't need to see him serve time. I needed him dead.

It was only after he was removed from the scene several minutes later that a female medic approached me. She took the coat off her body and draped it over me. I curled into a ball on the floor and cried. It was over. It was finally over.

I stayed in that position on the floor, unable to stop shaking as they asked me questions I wasn't able to answer. I must have been in shock. All I could do was shake.

At some point, they got bolt cutters and were able to remove the chain from my neck. Even then, I couldn't stop the shaking. While I knew I was safe, I didn't *feel* safe. More like a live wire that was about to explode.

That's when I felt a warm pair of arms lift me onto their lap. They cradled me like a baby. Instinctively, I curled into the warmth and inhaled a familiar scent.

My eyes opened as I looked up. "Malcolm?"

"Shh, it's okay, baby. I got you. You're safe now."

Blinking, I tried to wake up from what must have been a dream. "You're alive? Or am I dead too?"

Malcolm chuckled. "I'm alive. I'm not sure the same can be said about Connor, though. The EMTs said you got him pretty good. Well done. I'm so proud of you."

"But... how... how...?" I had a million questions but couldn't form any of them.

He pulled me closer to his chest. "We can talk about it all later. Right now, I just need you to get some rest. I've got you now."

I nodded as he lifted me off the floor. Malcolm was alive, and Connor was in custody. It didn't seem real.

"Kelli?" I asked. My voice broke.

"She's okay. She's with Holden. They're looking her over, but she seems to be okay."

"Is this really over?"

Malcolm nodded. "It is. We got the bastard. You're safe. And I am never letting you go. Deal?"

I let out a short hysterical laugh. "Deal."

"Now, let's get the hell out of here."

Closing my eyes, I let Malcolm carry me out of Hell. Again.

EPILOGUE

MALCOLM

For the first month after the raid, Amanda barely spoke. She mostly slept and would sit in a chair and stare off into space when awake. She only came out of her trance on days when Kelli stopped by. And sometimes even they didn't speak. They just held each other and wept over their shared trauma.

The trial was brutal. Seeing them both on the stand, forced to relive their stories in a packed courtroom, was an unthinkable cruelty. Connor, of course, pleaded not guilty, but against so many witnesses, there wasn't much even his Harvard Law attorney could defend him against. Connor didn't take the stand. He just sat there and watched Amanda like a hawk waiting to pounce.

It was only after Connor's sentencing to ten years behind bars, a sentence he likely paid to get as it was not nearly enough, that Amanda seemed to break free of whatever was latched onto her. It was almost as though she were holding her breath, disbelieving this was over until the words came out of the judge's mouth. Only then did she agree to go to therapy and see a doctor.

She wasn't eating well, and her sleep cycles were a mess. I was hoping the doctor would prescribe a sleeping pill and maybe hook her up with a nutritionist who could help her get back on track after so long of irregular feeding schedules.

"Will you come with me?" Amanda asked on the morning of her appointment.

"Of course."

She was still nervous to leave the house. Not that I blamed her. I imagined we would all be on edge for a while. Amanda was staying with me, and Kelli was still at Holden's as a temporary arrangement. But it didn't take much to see there would be nothing temporary about it. They were bonded now for life. They needed each other. Just like I needed Amanda.

At the doctors, they ran a whole series of tests. They took her blood and urine, checked her weight, height, and ran a string of tests for STDs. Who knew what Connor might have had?

As we waited in the room for the doctor to come back, Amanda twisted her hands along the edge of her hospital gown. The paper beneath her crinkled as she shifted her weight nervously.

"You okay?" I asked.

"That's what we're here to find out, right?"

The doctor came in then. We both sat up straight.

"So? How is she looking?"

The smile the doctor wore told me I didn't have to worry.

"All her tests came back normal. Her weight is low, but that's not uncommon at this stage. The weight will come on once the morning sickness stops. Usually in the second trimester."

"Morning sickness?" I asked.

I glanced down at Amanda, who didn't say anything. She just stared at the wall across the room, as though this was exactly the news she was dreading.

"She's pregnant?"

The doctor seemed confused. "Oh, I'm sorry. I thought that's what you were here for. I'm so sorry. The string of tests we did is common with a first prenatal visit, so I just assumed..."

Amanda let loose a shaky breath. She looked like she might pass out.

"Um, Doctor, could you give us a minute?"

"Of course. Just open the door when you're ready for me to come back." The doctor gave Amanda a sympathetic look before she left us alone.

There was no question as to who the father was. We had used a condom.

"Let me guess, Connor didn't wear protection?" There was no blame in my tone, just acceptance.

"He didn't need to. He would always pull out or..."

"Or?"

"Force me to take a Plan B after."

"So then, maybe it's not his?" The hope that filled my voice was evident but temporary.

"He didn't always remember to give me a pill. Or, later on, remember to pull out." Tears welled in her eyes as she grappled with her new reality. This would explain why she'd been so quiet. She must have known or at least suspected this might be the outcome. That was why she wanted me here: to see my reaction.

I ran my fingers through my hair and paced the tiny room. I wanted to throw something I was so angry at Connor, but I knew I had to keep my cool. Especially now.

"Okay... so now we know. It's still early, right? There's time to decide what you want to do."

She turned to look at me. "What I want to *do*?"

"You don't have to bear his child, Amanda. You can get an abortion. I will support you."

"You'll support me as long as I don't have his baby, you mean." Her voice was distant. Vacant. She was spiraling.

My teeth ground together. The idea of her bearing Connor's child was almost too much to think about. "No. That's not what I said, Amanda. Of course, I'll support you no matter what you choose. If you want to have the baby, then we can go buy a crib today. Hell, if you want to go the adoption route, that's fine too. Whatever you want to do, I'll support you."

Her tear-filled eyes looked up at me. Her bottom lip quivered. "What if I don't know what I want to do?" she whispered.

"That's okay too."

I pulled her in for a hug, and together we wept for the past and for the future. Even from his jail cell, Connor was still fucking with our lives.

In the end, Amanda decided to keep the baby. We bought a crib that very same day. As promised. She was in her fifth month of pregnancy and absolutely glowing. Despite it all, the pregnancy seemed to have helped her turn a corner, as if determined to make sure our child had the best life. Yes, *our* child. I would be that child's father, no matter what any biological test said. That baby was going to have my last name. We were going to be a family. And nothing Connor could do from his cell would stop that.

Therapy had been going well too. She and Kelli had a joint session a few times a month, and then she had a weekly session that did wonders for her mental health.

Kelli and Holden were getting stronger too. He was back on the force, and Kelli worked at a local animal shelter, caring for abused pets. Fitting. Holden and I still talked. He was determined to find his sister in Vincent's sex ring. If anyone could do it, it was him.

Amanda's black hair dye from our time on the run had all grown out, and her hair had been trimmed to cut out what evidence of that time remained. We had the nursery set up, and a wedding date set. Things couldn't have been more perfect.

"Okay, I'm off to therapy," Amanda said, coming from the bedroom. Her belly made it out the door before her. He was going to be a big baby, if her tummy was already this large.

"Let me grab my keys." I got up from my seat to approach her.

"Don't be silly. It's been five months, Malcolm. I need to start being able to do things on my own again."

"Yeah, but babe, you're sooo pregnant. Do you think you can touch the pedals?" I kissed her gently on the nose.

"Har, har. I'll be fine. My therapist said I need to start being more independent. To prove to myself that there isn't danger lurking in every corner."

I let loose a deep sigh. She was right. This was something she needed to be able to do. She had to be able to feel safe doing things alone. It didn't mean I liked it. I huffed. "Ugh. Fine. But if you get nervous, or anxious—"

"I know. I'll call you." She stood up on her tiptoes as her belly pushed against mine, and she placed a tender kiss on me.

"I'll be back in an hour or so."

"Okay. I'm proud of you." And I was. This was a good thing. For everyone.

CONNOR

Two surgeries, three weeks in recovery from Amanda's attempt to take out my spleen, one awful trial, and five months later, and I was still no closer to getting out of this place. My attorney had fought hard, but there was too much evidence against me. He said I should be grateful it's only ten years. Little did he know I paid for that reduction in time. Without my bribe, it would have been life without parole. And that was on me. I'd gotten sloppy. Been greedy. But worst of all, I trusted a woman.

Since being inside, I'd been making as many connections as I could, but with limited access to my funds to pay people off, it was proving rather difficult. I'd figure it out, but it was taking far longer than I was comfortable with.

"Brooks, you got a visitor," a guard said as he banged against my cell with his cuffs. The noise echoed in my ears.

Must be my attorney. Maybe he'd finally found a way out of this mess. I stood up and let the guard cuff me through the bars. Once I was securely bound, the guard opened the door and led me to the visiting rooms. A pane of secured glass separated prisoners from visitors.

A handful of men were talking to their loved ones on the black phone, which connected them to the outside world. Pathetic, really.

The guard brought me to the last spot on the visitor's row, and when I sat down, I was floored to discover that it was not my attorney sitting across the glass, but Amanda.

What the fuck?

Without my consent, my heart nearly leaped out of my chest.

She looked absolutely radiant. Her red hair was back, cut short in a pixie cut. Her lush red lips were tinted with a light rose color, but it was her eyes that captivated me. A mix of fear and hope?

The phone was already in her hand as I sat there dumbfounded. She seemed anxious to talk to me. About what?

"Ya got five minutes, Brooks," the guard said, taking one step back to give me some sense of privacy. Of which there was none here.

Lifting the phone beside me, I pressed it to my ear.

"Amanda... what are you doing here?"

"Does cancer run in your family?" she said without preamble.

"Cancer?" What the hell was she talking about?

"What about diabetes? Any heart disease?"

I blinked several times at her, utterly confused. "Family history? Why on earth—"

That's when I saw her free hand gently touch her stomach. A stomach I was only now noticing was rather pronounced.

"You're pregnant."

"Yes. I ask again, are there any medical issues in your family that I need to know about?"

More blinking. "You think it's mine?"

Amanda cleared her throat. "I don't think. I know. Now, can you please answer my questions? The doctors need to know the father's medical history, and I don't know what to tell them."

"This isn't possible. I pulled out. I gave you Plan B—" *Wait...*

Did I always? We had a lot of sex. *Shit*. She was pregnant. With *my* child. "How far along are you?"

"A little over five months. Please, we don't have much time, and this is really important."

I leaned in and pressed my hand to the glass. "Why didn't you get an abortion?"

Amanda sat up straighter. "It's not his fault that his father is a monster."

"*His*. It's a boy?"

"Yes. Now, will you please—"

"Just a little alcoholism and narcissistic tendencies and, oh, psychotic behavior runs in the family. But you knew that."

"Thank you." She went to put the phone down.

"Amanda, wait. Does Malcolm know you came to see me?"

"No. And he doesn't need to." That's when I saw the massive rock on her left finger.

"Are you married?"

She looked at her ring. "Engaged. We're going to get married next year. In the sanctuary where Holden and Kelli hid. Malcolm bought it. He's renovating it. Once it's ready, we'll be married."

"How quaint."

"Goodbye, Connor."

"You don't fool me, Amanda." She froze where she was. "I know the real reason you kept the baby. You wanted to hold onto a piece of me. As twisted as this all is, you still can't let me go. Isn't that right, Amanda?"

Amanda leaned closer to the glass. Her eyes held a hint of challenge. "Enjoy your cage, Connor."

With that, she hung up the phone, pushed out of the chair, and left.

A huge grin spread across my lips.

I was going to be a father. I'd have an heir for my empire.

Once I got out of here, the three of us would be able to start over. I'd do it right this time. I'd hide us where no one could find us. We'd be a perfect family like I always imagined I could have.

I watched in glee as the door shut behind Amanda. There was euphoria at knowing that our time together wasn't over, but that it was merely going to be postponed for a while until my attorneys found an eventual loophole and got me out early. In the meantime, I could plan. I would use my captive time wisely, as my mother had always taught me.

"Let's go." The guard kicked at my chair. I stood up and beamed at him. This was a very good day.

"Oh, one last thing," the guard said as he checked my restraints. He lowered his lips to my ear. "Vincent sends his regards."

I recoiled as the guard smiled. He walked over to the cell door for the holding pen and let five inmates approach me. Each held a makeshift shive in their hands.

"You have two minutes. Do your worst, boys. I didn't see a thing." The guard grinned as he turned toward the wall to have deniability.

That was when the first jab came. Then another from behind. Then a third. A fourth. I didn't feel the fifth. Then after the sixth, I didn't feel anything.

Thank you for reading! Did you enjoy? Please add your review because nothing helps an author more and encourages readers to take a chance on a book than a review.

And don't miss another dark romance and psychological thriller mix from Danielle Bannister with GIRL ON FIRE available now. Turn the page for a sneak peek!

You can also sign up for the City Owl Press newsletter to receive notice of all book releases!

SNEAK PEEK OF GIRL ON FIRE

California. That's where I decided I was going to start my life over. It seemed like a good place to disappear into the masses. As good as any, I supposed. I had gotten it into my head that once I turned eighteen, things were going to get better. I'd be an adult. I'd be, I don't know, smarter somehow.

It wasn't the first time I'd run away from home, but it was sure as hell going to be the last. I couldn't stay there. Not anymore. I knew leaving meant I'd have to hitch rides again, something I wasn't looking forward to. But nothing in life is free, especially not a lift from a trucker.

By the time I'd made it to Indiana, my soul was about as low as it could get. That's where Al found me. I was sitting outside a convenience store, sizing up the truckers as they stopped to fuel up, and wondering which one would be the least cruel to a hitcher. It was hard to gauge most of the time. The ones that looked the nicest often were the most sadistic.

Al didn't say anything to me. He just stopped in front of me and handed me a Sprite and a Snickers bar. I looked up at him, my guard raised even though he looked like a hillbilly Santa. He wore a dirty white T-shirt, red suspenders, and a bright neon camo hat.

"Looks like you could use these more than I could," he said.

"Thanks." I hadn't eaten for far too long, and I was hungry. I tore into the bar with the vigor of an animal, which is what I felt like. I had some money on me, but I tried never to spend it—only when starvation seemed imminent.

"You need a lift somewhere, missy?" he asked. I saw what

appeared to be genuine kindness. You can tell a lot about a person by the eyes. His were pinched in a smile, not narrowed like a hunter sizing up his prey. That look I knew all too well. Still, he was a stranger, so I didn't answer at first, mostly because I was chewing, but I was also wondering just how safe he'd be.

"You remind me of my daughter," he said. "She would have been eighteen this year." His lips curled inward at an unpleasant memory. He had a dead kid. He struck me as the protective grandpa-type.

"Where you headed?" I asked.

"Mullen, Nebraska."

I stood up. "Well, sure beats the hell out of this place." I met his eye. "What's your price?"

"My price?" he asked, eyebrows shooting toward the sky.

"For the ride?"

His gaze softened, as though understanding what I was asking.

"How about you just help unload the truck when we get there, and we call it square." He hitched his thumb toward his truck.

"What's in it, dead bodies?"

He chuckled. "Well, I guess that's the gamble you'll have to take if you want the lift."

I looked back at the truck again. It had no logos or markings that would give any indication of what was inside. I chewed on my lip and scanned the other lingering truckers before deciding.

"My name's Sarah," I said, holding out my hand.

"I'm Al. Al King. Pleasure to meet you."

Of course, in retrospect, I should have told him, "No, thanks," and taken my chances on another lift, but he seemed like a decent guy, and unknowingly or not, I really needed something decent in my life.

"So what's Mullen known for?" I asked the second day on the road. The breakfast he'd bought for me still weighed heavy in my stomach. I'd forgotten what a real meal had felt like. While he had paid the tab, I had tucked two of the leftover biscuits into my bag to savor later.

"Oh, well, Mullen is a small town, so aside from cattle, probably The Sandhills," Al replied with unmistakable pride.

"What's that? A restaurant?" I asked.

"The Sandhills is more of an area of land than one set place. They're basically grass-covered sand dunes. Awful pretty to look at. A might finer than out there," he said, pointing to the vastness. I followed his gesture and glanced over the static view. We'd been driving for hours without coming across a single bump or curve in the road, not even in the landscape around it. It appeared like we were never making any forward progress but instead, frozen in this part of the world, forever.

"So you have cattle and green sand. Sounds awesome," I muttered.

He laughed a deep, raspy laugh, the kind of laugh you get from years of smoking, although I didn't see the remnants of cigarette butts in his ashtray—only loose change. I frowned, wishing he did smoke. I never smoked, but man, I loved to watch those embers burn.

"We have our fun," he said.

I turned my head and rolled my eyes. "Sure."

"You just wait until you see what you're unloading tomorrow, darlin'."

I let out a breath. "Can't wait."

Al's smile shifted a bit. I got the sense he was going to start fishing for information soon. So far, he hadn't said much, as though knowing I wasn't going to speak until I was ready, if at all. But it was clear he had reached a point where the inquiries would begin.

"Mind if I ask how old you are?" He started with an easy one.

I got that question a lot. Most of the time if I got asked how old I was it was because the guy wanted to know if I was legal or not, which most of the time I hadn't been. With Al, I got the feeling that he was just curious, so I told the truth. "I'll be nineteen this month," I said, picking at my nails. They were caked in filth and never seemed to get clean.

Al glanced over at me. "When?"

"Friday the 13th, of course."

Al laughed. "Aren't you the lucky one?"

I stared at the horizon. "Cursed is more like it."

We didn't talk for a few minutes, which was fine. It was easy riding with Al. Perhaps that's why I didn't ditch him at breakfast that morning. My normal rule was one day. Any more than that and you risked forming an unhealthy bond that even the nice ones had a hard time resisting, but something told me Al wasn't like the others.

"Sarah. You got a last name?" His beady eyes squinted as he smiled.

"Brickle." I realized after I said it that I probably shouldn't have. No one had asked or even cared what my last name was, so it sort of slipped out before I could take it back.

"Brickle? Interesting surname."

I yawned. "Yeah, it's actually dying out. I'm sure my mom was pissed at me for not being a boy so I could carry out the legacy." I scoffed. One hell of a legacy that would be.

He laughed but didn't let the subject drop as I'd hoped. "What about the rest of your family? Got some out this way, do you? Heading for a visit?" I could hear the skepticism in his voice. So far, I had managed to keep our limited conversations away from my past.

"Nope," I said, pulling my knees to my chest. I had already kicked off my shoes, so I flexed my feet a bit, enjoying the coolness of the cab.

He nodded, as though he expected as much.

"Your mom know you're out here?"

I let loose a short breath. I'd better nip this conversation before it escalated. "I had a mom. She was a meth addict. She died. My dad left when I was two. No other family. End of story, okay?"

If he was shocked by my bluntness, he didn't show it.

"Can I ask one last question? And then, I promise, I'll stop pestering you." I could feel Al's eyes flick over to me, waiting, so I rubbed my forehead as permission.

"What are you running from?"

"Honestly?" I asked.

He kept his eyes on the road but nodded.

I laid my head back against the seat and closed my eyes. "Myself."

"Damn hard thing to hide from for long," he said simply.

I stretched my arms back and gave a hearty yawn. "Don't I know it."

I wasn't tired so much as I was bored. I was getting antsy. I dug into my bag on the floor and pulled out a small wad of cash. I'd learned a long time ago to never hold it all in one place. I had forty bucks in my shoe, six in my jeans, and a ten spot in my bra. The backpack I'd lifted from the trash only held a few bills and a bit of loose change. I'm not proud of the services I had to provide to get what little money I had, but at least I wasn't a drug addict throwing it all away. I was being frugal and saving everything I possibly could for that reset button in California.

I fished free six single bills and pressed them as flat as I could on the leg of my pants then placed them in the cup holder next to Al.

"For breakfast, earlier," I said. I'd never eaten in a truck stop diner until that morning. "And for letting me sleep in the cab last night," I added, placing another dollar in with the others.

"Keep your money," he said.

I shook my head. "No, I owe you. It's not much, I know, but take it. Please."

"It seems like you could use that money more than I could."

I glanced over at him. He wasn't saying it to be hurtful, but rather as a way of understanding. I sensed he'd find a way to sneak it back into my bag if I didn't take it, so I relented. Letting out a breath, I grabbed the money and slid it back inside.

"You know, when I was about your age, I stole a car," Al said.

My eyes narrowed in disbelief. He didn't seem the type for grand theft auto.

"My old man's car," he continued.

I frowned. "Well, that's not really the same thing."

"He was the sheriff at the time."

I laughed. "Not smart."

Al was watching the road, but his eyes looked far away, lost in thought. "After he cooled down, he asked me why I stole it. I shrugged and said, 'I needed to get to Annabel's place.'" He smiled. "She's my wife now, see, but back then, I was smitten, and I needed to see her every minute of every day. I told him, 'I needed that car so I could go see her.'" His smile faded a bit. "He said, 'Son, you don't need a car. You need a job. A car is just a thing, but a job gives you the freedom to choose your path.'"

I nodded politely because that seemed like what he wanted me to do.

"Do you have a job? Waiting out there for ya, that is?" he asked.

I snorted. "I don't even have a path." It was meant to sound funny, but instead, it came out terribly sad.

Al pursed up his lips like he was thinking about how he could save my soul. I shook my head, amused.

"Look, I appreciate the lift, but I know what you're trying to do."

He peeked over at me, one bushy white eyebrow lifted high. "What's that, now?"

"I don't need your advice." I blinked. "I don't need anything. Or anyone." I said those words too low for him to hear. "After I unload whatever is on this truck, I'll be out of your hair."

Al surprised me by laughing. "So you want to remain an enigma, huh? Well, that's all fine and good, I suppose." He turned his attention to me for a moment. "I didn't listen to my father when he lectured me either." His expression was kind, but I could tell he was upset. "See, the thing is I have got myself in a bit of a pickle."

"A pickle?" I snickered.

"Of sorts. My oldest son, Brad, well, he just graduated from the police academy." Al smiled. "He takes after his grandpa." The smile faded from his face. "But he's going to be moving to

Boston next week to start work and won't be around over the summer to help like he used to. I was hoping I'd be able to help Kyle this year instead, but Annabel's taken ill, the kind of sick you don't just bounce back from..." His eyes began to well up. "She needs me, see, and I can't afford to hire someone to help him."

"Who's Kyle?"

Big Al's eyes cleared as he gave me a proud grin. "He's my youngest. Just turned nineteen. Boy is smart as a tack but stubborn as a mule. He should be in college, making something of himself, but he's insisted on staying on to take after the cattle and his mother when I go on runs." He sighed. "Claims we'd never make it if he left too."

"Would you?" I asked, already sensing his answer.

Al's eyes grew dark. "No. Probably not."

"He's not stubborn then, just smart," I offered. "Like you said."

He gave me a thin smile. "Too smart for his own good." Al took a deep inhalation as he stared down the long road that ran far into the never-ending horizon. "I can't keep on like this much longer. Truckin' is hard on your body, worse on your mind."

"Amen to that," I said, shifting positions for the hundredth time since breakfast.

He was still peering at the horizon. A heavy burden weighed on his mind, so I sat and waited for him to compose himself. It wasn't a time for talking. I had a sneaking suspicion he was gearing up to ask me to help him, and I wasn't sure how I was going to answer.

"Look, Sarah, I'll be straight with you." Al turned on his blinker and slowly eased off the highway, flicking on his hazards before he parked the rig. He turned to face me. "I know we just met, but I have a way of telling a bad seed from a good one," he started.

I held up my hand in protest. "Let me stop you right there, Al." I tucked a chunk of my dark hair around my ear; hair that I relied on in the past to mask my face, but here, it felt like he needed to be clear on who I really was. I needed him to see the real me.

"You're sweet and all, but I'm not who you think I am. I'm one of the bad seeds."

He scoffed. "Nah, you just haven't been given the right soil to grow in, that's all."

Such a simple statement, but one that tried to take root in my soul nevertheless. If only that were true... My eyes glazed over with emotion for half a second. I had to swallow the thickness forming in my throat. I'd be damned if he was gonna make me cry.

"Come work for me," he said. "Just for the summer, if you like. I can give you room and board," he said, shifting to face me better, "and a ride to California." At that, I looked up at him. "I go out in late September...I'd be happy to bring you along."

All of my instincts told me to turn him down, to resist the temptation of feeling like I was needed somewhere, if only for a few months. But, of course, I didn't. I told him I would help him, just for the summer. Little did I know that I had effectively set the wheels in motion—wheels that could never be stopped once I had laid eyes on Kyle.

Don't stop now. Keep reading with your copy of GIRL ON FIRE today!

And don't miss more from Danielle Bannister. Stay up to date on all of her release information, cover reveals, sales, and giveaways by joining her newsletter.

Want even more from Danielle Bannister? Read GIRL ON FIRE and be sure to sign-up to receive all the news and updates.

Fire was my only companion. A burning light in a world otherwise filled with darkness. A life of pain and abuse I never thought I'd escape.

I'm still not convinced I have.

When friendly Santa-figure turned trucker, Al, finds me at a rest stop and offers me a job at his idyllic farm in small-town Nebraska, the picturesque family life is more than I could hope for.

And his youngest son, Kyle, is a dream romance that I don't deserve.

But no dream lasts. As a new nightmare begins, I'm back where I started. Captive. Abandoned. Alone. And staring into the flames.

Except this time the embers are dying, and when the monster in the dark enslaves my soul, no one will stoke me back to life.

If you like a survivor story with a touch of romance, you will love this beautiful dark psychological thriller.

Please sign up for the City Owl Press newsletter for chances to win special subscriber-only contests and giveaways as well as receiving information on upcoming releases and special excerpts.

All reviews are **welcome** and **appreciated**. Please consider leaving one on your favorite social media and book buying sites.

Escape Your World. Get Lost in Ours! www.cityowlpress.com

ACKNOWLEDGMENTS

There were two sets of eyes on this third book when it was in pretty rough shape. They saw the bones of the story and helped me build the muscle. To Angela Domenichelli and Cassy Bunnell, I am so grateful for your willingness to read this in draft form to help make it into the book it is today.

ABOUT THE AUTHOR

DANIELLE BANNISTER lives with her two children in Mid-Coast Maine, along with her precious coffee pot and peppermint mocha creamer. She holds a BA in Theater from the University of Southern Maine and her Masters in Literary Education from the University of Orono.

When she's not on the stage or on the page, you'll find her drinking tea and binge-watching all the Netflix. As one does.

www.daniellebannister.com

facebook.com/BannisterBooks
x.com/dbannisterbooks
instagram.com/daniellebannisterbooks
pinterest.com/bannisterbooks
bookbub.com/authors/danielle-bannister
tiktok.com/@daniellebannisterbooks

ABOUT THE PUBLISHER

City Owl Press is a cutting edge indie publishing company, bringing the world of romance and speculative fiction to discerning readers.

Escape Your World. Get Lost in Ours!

www.cityowlpress.com

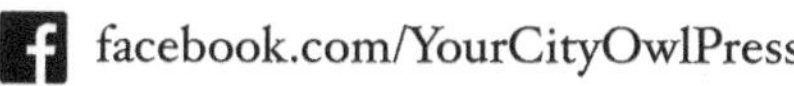

facebook.com/YourCityOwlPress
x.com/cityowlpress
instagram.com/cityowlbooks
pinterest.com/cityowlpress

www.ingramcontent.com/pod-product-compliance
Lightning Source LLC
LaVergne TN
LVHW091146080826
845145LV00008B/2274

* 9 7 8 1 6 4 8 9 8 5 4 4 7 *